Alice and the Boy who Slew the Jabberwock

Alice and the Boy who Slew the Jabberwock

A Tale inspired by Lewis Carroll's *Wonderland*

by

Allan William Parkes

POEMS BY
LEWIS CARROLL

ILLUSTRATIONS BY
HARRY FURNISS AND
HARRY ROUNTREE

evertype

2016

Published by Evertype, 73 Woodgrove, Portlaoise, R32 ENP6, Ireland. *www.evertype.com*.

A catalogue record for this book is available from the British Library.

ISBN-10 1-78201-184-6
ISBN-13 978-1-78201-184-2

Typeset in De Vinne Text, Mona Lisa, ENGRAVERS' ROMAN, and *Liberty* by Michael Everson.

Edited by Michael Everson.

Illustrations, some edited by Michael Everson (†) and Allan William Parkes (‡):
John Tenniel, 1871, *Through the Looking-Glass*, frontispiece.
Harry Furniss, 1889, *Sylvie and Bruno*, pp. 14† (window), 28, 29 (both), 30, 31, 43, 44, 46 (badgers), 50, 51, 55†, 62†, 74, 111†.
——, 1893, *Sylvie and Bruno Concluded*, pp. 11, 12, 13, 18, 20 (both), 21, 27†, 57, 63, 64, 65, 90†, 121.
——, 1908-1909, *Alice's Adventures in Wonderland*, pp. 5† (Alice), 6, 7 (both), 8, 14† (Alice), 23, 24, 25, 26†, 32, 34†, 36, 37, 41, 46 (quadrille), 48‡, 75†, 88†, 102†, 103, 107†, 115† (both), 117, 125†, 126†.
Harry Rountree, c. 1925, *Alice's Adventures in Wonderland*, pp. 68†, 83†, 89†, 101, 113†. © Estate of Harry Rountree.
——, c. 1928, *Through the Looking-Glass*, pp. 5 (cat), 9†, 58†, 79†, 85†, 93†, 99†, 100†, 109†, 114†, 122†, 127. © Estate of Harry Rountree.

Cover: Michael Everson.

Printed by LightningSource.

Foreword

One day the thought occurred to me: Why should the splendid jokes and poems strewn throughout Lewis Carroll's gigantic novel *Sylvie and Bruno* languish ignored and forgotten, when they could be put into the mouths of the Alice characters we all know and love? After all, the same wit and humour underpins them.

And so, Carpenter-like, I began sawing and assembling; and, Walrus-like, began selecting the oysters of nonsense of the largest size. And now in your hands you hold the result.

By using the Key found in *Sylvie and Bruno* the door has been opened for a new adventure for Alice. A new *Alice* book that is 95% pure Carroll.

Allan William Parkes
Cradley Heath, February 2016

Alice and the Boy
who Slew the Jabberwock

Contents

I. Welcome to Wonderland 5
II. "A Pig-Tale" 17
III. "He Thought He Saw" 27
IV. The Gryphon and the Mock
Turtle 39
V. The Knight is Old 54
VI. The Knight is Young 61
VII. The Lecture is Introduced 72
VIII. A Mad Lecture 87
IX. Three Experiments 93
X. The Banquet 100
XI. Her Imperial Fatness 114
XII. Good-night, Wonderland 120

Faces in the Fire

The night creeps onward, sad and slow:
In these red embers' dying glow
The forms of Fancy come and go—

Sunk is the last faint flickering blaze:
The vision of departed days
Is vanished even as I gaze.

The pictures, with their ruddy light,
Are changed to dust and ashes white,
And I am left alone with night.

CHAPTER I

Welcome to Wonderland

Alice sat on the hearthrug in front of the fire, playing with her cat. The cat wore a cravat round its neck made of ribbon. This had been applied by Alice herself, and had taken some time and not a little difficulty. The cat had wriggled so much she'd had to tie the bow to the back of his neck instead of the front, so she wasn't really satisfied with the result. Then she had played a game of rolling a ball to and fro with him, but though he had played willingly enough at first, he had now lost all interest in the activity.

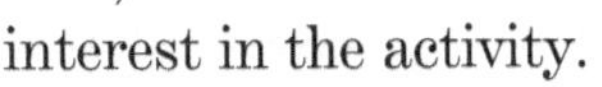

The tiles around the fireplace were covered with pictures of birds.

There was a blue-and-grey pelican—or was it a dodo? There was a green owl with bright yellow eyes catching a mouse. There was a heron feeding a fish to a dolphin. There was a blue gryphon. There was a red bird that resembled a winged serpent. There was a green bird with tail-feathers like a peacock. There was a large blue bird about to eat—or speak to—a smaller blue one. There was a green-and-blue bird among a tangle of green leaves. There were eight blue-coloured birds with curious beaks and large eyes all crowded on one tile.

"It's fortunate those birds aren't real," said Alice severely to her cat. "Or you'd try to catch them, wouldn't you? If there's one thing you like more than little mice it's little birds. But they don't like you, do they? And I ca'n't say I blame them."

Only two tiles had no birds on them. A red bear (with a badly chipped head from an accident with a fire-iron) occupied one. A very strange red porcupine occupied the other.

The lonely evening seemed long and tedious: yet Alice lingered on, watching the dying fire, and letting Fancy mould the red embers into the forms and faces belonging to bygone scenes.

Most of the coals were small and white, but some large ones still glowed brightly, and sometimes flared up suddenly and unexpectedly.

Watching a coal burn smaller and smaller, she remembered how she had shrunk in size under the glass table, after drinking from the bottle labelled "DRINK ME".

Watching a flame shoot upwards, she remembered how she had grown in height, after eating a cake marked in currants "EAT ME".

A space among the coals reminded her of the little room in the White Rabbit's house, where *another* magic bottle had made her grow uncomfortably large. But then, briefly, she saw something not in her memory of the little room at all.

The White Rabbit's face appeared at his window and looked directly at her!

How extraordinary! Was it out of the fire or out of Wonderland itself?

Then, as a falling coal sent up a fountain of flying sparks, she saw the pack of cards—full of angry faces and accusing fingers—rising up and falling over her.

And following the White Rabbit and the pack of cards, other faces began to appear.

Now it seemed to be the Cheshire-Cat's grin that sparkled for a moment, and died away: now it was Tweedledum and Tweedledee's rosy cheeks: and now Humpty Dumpty's jolly round face, beaming with delight.

"Welcome to Wonderland, my little one!" he seemed to say. And then the glowing coal, which for the moment embodied the dear old white shape of Humpty Dumpty, began to wax dim, and with its dying lustre the words seemed to die away into silence. Alice seized the poker, and with an artful touch or two revived the waning glow, while Fancy sang to her once again the magic strain she loved to hear.

"Welcome to Wonderland, my little one," the cheery voice repeated. "I told them you were coming. Your rooms are all ready for you. And the Red Queen and the White Queen—well, I think they're rather pleased than otherwise! In fact her Majesty the White Queen said 'I hope she'll be in time for the Queen of Hearts' Birthday Party!' Those were her very words, I assure you! It'll be a jolly banquet, now *you've* come, dear. I *am* so glad to see you again!"

She soon lost her lonely feeling in the hearty welcome her old friend gave her, and the cozy warmth and cheerful light of the little sitting-room in which she stood.

"Little, as you see, but quite enough for us two. Now, take the easy-chair, old fellow, and let's have another look at you!"

"I'm afraid I've been very long in coming," Alice remarked politely.

"Well, yes," Humpty Dumpty assented. "However, you're very short now you're come: that's *some* comfort."

Alice sat down in the chair (which had a walking-stick leaning against it) and looked around her. The walls were covered with tapestries depicting all the King's horses and all the King's men, and a suit of armour (presumably belonging to one of them) stood in a corner. At her feet was a tiled fireplace not unlike the one she had left behind, only the tiles here were a blank white, as if all the little birds had flown away.

Humpty Dumpty was recuperating from his fall sitting in an armchair, supported by pillows, and with an open dictionary in front of him.

He sighed. "My poor head," he said sadly. "It got quite a shock! All the King's men couldn't get me on the wall again. My head is too weak to balance. As for inventing extra meanings for words, that is *quite* out of the question. I have to be content with the meanings they already have. I've been reading this dictionary for eighteen hours and three quarters, and now I shall rest for fourteen minutes and a half." He shut up the book so quickly he caught his nose in it. "Ouch!" he said, then added: "Recite something soothing for me while I rest."

Alice folded her hands together, and perhaps because she was still puzzling over where the "little birds" might have gone, these words came from her lips:—

> *Little Birds are dining*
> *Warily and well*
> *Hid in mossy cell:*
> *Hid, I say, by waiters*
> *Gorgeous in their gaiters—*
> *I've a tale to tell.*

Little Birds are feeding
  Justices with jam,
    Rich in frizzled ham:
Rich, I say, in oysters
Haunting shady cloisters—
    That is what I am.

Little Birds are teaching
  Tigresses to smile,
    Innocent of guile:
Smile, I say, not smirkle—
Mouth a semicircle,
    That's the proper style!

Little Birds are sleeping
  All among the pins
    Where the loser wins:
Where, I say, he sneezes
When and how he pleases
    So the Tale begins.

Little Birds are writing
Interesting books,
To be read by cooks:
Read, I say, not roasted—
Letterpress, when toasted,
Loses its good looks.

Little Birds are playing
Bagpipes on the shore,
Where the tourists snore:
"Thanks!" they cry. "'Tis thrilling!
Take, oh take this shilling!
Let us have no more."

Little Birds are bathing
Crocodiles in cream,
Like a happy dream:
Like, but not so lasting—
Crocodiles, when fasting,
Are not all they seem!

Little Birds are seeking
   Hecatombs of haws,
   Dressed in snowy gauze:
Dressed, I say, in fringes
Half alive with hinges—
   Thus they break the laws.

Little Birds are choking
   Baronets with bun
   Taught to fire a gun:
Taught, I say, to splinter
Salmon in the winter—
   Merely for the fun.

Little Birds are hiding
   Crimes in carpet-bags,
   Blessed by happy stags:
Blessed, I say, though beaten—
Since our friends are eaten
   When the memory flags.

Little Birds are tasting
Gratitude and gold,
Pale with sudden cold:
Pale, I say, and wrinkled—
When the bells have tinkled,
And the Tale is told.

Humpty Dumpty had paid less and less attention to the recitation as she went on, and by the time she'd finished he was looking out of the window as if something had attracted his attention.

"What are you looking at?" asked Alice, joining him.

"Don't interrupt!" he said as she approached. "I'm counting the sheep in the field!"

"How many are there?" she enquired.

"About a thousand and four," said Humpty Dumpty.

"You mean 'about a thousand,'" Alice corrected him. "There's no good saying '*and four*': you ca'n't be sure about the four!"

"And you're as wrong as ever!" Humpty Dumpty exclaimed triumphantly. "It's just the four I *can* be sure about; 'cause they're here, grubbling under the window! It's the *thousand* I'm not perfectly sure about!"

"But some of them have gone into the sheepfold," Alice said, looking out of the window at the small white shapes.

"Yes," said Humpty Dumpty: "but they went so slowly and so fewly, I didn't care to count *them*."

"Why do you need so many?"

"To make lighter and lighter wool. Let me explain," he added, seeing Alice's look of surprise. "Suppose you desire a race of *pigeons* of a particular shape or colour, do you not select, from year to year, those that are nearest to the shape or colour you want, and keep those, and part with the others?"

"We do," Alice agreed.

"Exactly so. I have applied the same process," he continued, "to many other purposes. I have gone on selecting *walking-sticks*—always keeping those that walked *best*—till I expect one day to obtain some that can walk by themselves! I am selecting lighter and lighter wool, till I expect one day to obtain some that will be lighter than air!"

"What would you use it for?" asked Alice.

"Well, one use would be for packing articles, to go by parcel post. It would make them weigh *less than nothing*, you know."

"And how would the Post Office know what you have to pay?"

"That would be the beauty of the new system!" Humpty Dumpty cried exultingly. "They would pay *me*: I wouldn't pay *them*! I expect to get as much as five shillings for sending a parcel."

"But doesn't your Government object to such a plan?"

"Well, they *do* object a little. They say it would get so expensive, in the long run. But the thing's as clear as daylight, by their own rules. If I send a parcel, that weighs a pound *more* than nothing, I *pay* threepence: so, of course, if it weighs a pound *less* than nothing, I ought to *receive* threepence."

"That would *indeed* be useful!" admitted Alice.

"Another use," Humpty Dumpty continued, "would be to make articles of *clothing*. No one would ever drown at sea, for it would make them lighter than water. If my cravat had been made of such wool, my fall off the wall would have been far less heavy, and all the King's horses and all the King's men would have been more comfortable carrying me back than if they'd carried nothing at all. The only disadvantage would be the danger of floating away altogether."

CHAPTER II

"A Pig-Tale"

Humpty Dumpty looked seriously at Alice. "I know a poem about someone who would, like myself, definitely have found such clothing useful. Would you like to hear it?"

"Certainly," said Alice.

"The title is *'The Tale of a Pig'*—I mean *'A Pig-Tale'*," he corrected himself. "It has Introductory Verses at the beginning, and at the end."

"It ca'n't have Introductory Verses at the *end*, can it?" said Alice.

"Wait till you hear it," said Humpty Dumpty: "then you'll see. I'm not sure it hasn't some in the *middle*, as well."

> *There was a Pig that sat alone*
> *   Beside a ruined Pump:*
> *By day and night he made his moan—*
> *It would have stirred a heart of stone*
> *To see him wring his hoofs and groan,*
> *   Because he could not jump.*

A certain Camel heard him shout—
A Camel with a hump.
"Oh, is it Grief, or is it Gout?
What is this bellowing about?"
That Pig replied, with quivering snout,
"Because I cannot jump!"

That Camel scanned him, dreamy-eyed.
"Methinks you are too plump.
I never knew a Pig so wide—
That wobbled so from side to side—
Who could, however much he tried,
Do such a thing as JUMP!

"Yet mark those trees, two miles away,
All clustered in a clump:
If you could trot there twice a day,
Nor ever pause for rest or play,
In the far future—Who can say?—
You may be fit to jump."

That Camel passed, and left him there
　　Beside the ruined Pump.
Oh, horrid was that Pig's despair!
His shrieks of anguish filled the air.
He wrung his hoofs, he rent his hair.
　　Because he could not jump.

There was a Frog that wandered by—
　　A sleek and shining lump:
Inspected him with fishy aye,
And said "O Pig, what makes you cry?"
And bitter was that Pig's reply,
　　"Because I cannot jump!"

That Frog he grinned a grin of glee,
　　And hit his chest a thump.
"O Pig," he said, "be ruled by me,
And you shall see what you shall see.
This minute, for a trifling fee,
　　I'll teach you how to jump!

"You may be faint from many a fall,
　　And bruised with many a bump:
But, if you persevere through all,
And practise first on something small,
Concluding with a ten-foot wall,
　　You'll find that you CAN jump!"

That Pig looked up with joyful start:
　　"O Frog, you ARE a trump!
Your words have healed my inward smart—
Come, name your fee and do your part:
Bring comfort to a broken heart,
　　By teaching me to jump!"

"My fee shall be a mutton-chop,
    My goal this ruined Pump.
Observe with what an airy flop
I plant myself upon the top!
Now bend your knees and take a hop,
    For that's the way to jump!"

Uprose that Pig, and rushed, full whack,
    Against the ruined pump:
Rolled over like an empty sack,
And settled down upon his back,
While all his bones at once went "Crack!"
    It was a fatal jump.

When Humpty Dumpty had recited this verse, he went across to the fire-place, and put his head up the chimney. In doing this, he lost his balance, and fell head-first into the empty grate, and got so firmly fixed there that it was some time before he could be dragged out again.

"I just wanted to make sure no one was listening up the chimney," he explained.

"I'm so sorry you fell down," said Alice.

"I didn't fall *down*," he corrected. "I'm wider than I am tall, so I ca'n't fall *down*."

"You must have blacked your face in the grate," said Alice anxiously. "Let me send for some soap?"

"Thanks, no," said Humpty Dumpty, keeping his face turned away. "Black's quite a respectable colour. Besides, soap would be no use without water."

Keeping his back well turned away from Alice, he went on with his recitation:—

That Camel passed, as Day grew dim
  Around the ruined Pump.
"O broken heart! O broken limb!
It needs," that Camel said to him,
"Something more fairy-like and slim,
  To execute a jump!"

That Pig lay still as any stone,
  And could not stir a stump:
Nor ever, if the truth were known,
Was he again observed to moan,
Nor ever wring his hoofs and groan,
  Because he could not jump.

That Frog made no remark, for he
  Was dismal as a dump:
He knew the consequence must be
That he would never get his fee—
And still he sits, in miserie,
  Upon that ruined Pump!

"It' s a miserable story!" said Humpty Dumpty. "It begins miserably, and it ends miserablier. I think I shall cry. Please lend me your spare handkerchief."

"I don't have one with me, I'm afraid," said Alice.

"Then I wo'n't cry," said Humpty Dumpty manfully. "What are you going to give the Queen of Hearts for her birthday-present?" he enquired, suddenly changing the subject.

Alice looked in her pockets.

"What about this?" she said, producing a small silver pig witb a red cushion back. "Would she accept a second-hand pin-cushion? It cost me fourpence halfpenny. And the *pins* they gave me for nothing!"

Humpty Dumpty looked impressed.

He counted the pins. "Fifteen of 'em, and only one bent!" he said in a voice of high glee. "That would be *perfect*. Her Majesty could make the bent one into a *hook*! To catch the Knave of Hearts with, when he runs away with the tarts!

"The fourteen and a half minutes is up!" He opened the dictionary again. "Five minutes per poem and four and a half minutes general conversation. Good-bye! I'll join you at the Banquet later."

"But how do I get there?"

"Oh, you will simply pass from one room to another till you get there, you know. I'm constantly coming on new rooms and passages, and very seldom succeed in finding the old ones again. Just be careful which doors you go through. For instance, there's the rabbit-hutch and the hall-clock. One gets a little confused with *them*—both having doors, you know. Now, only yesterday—would you believe it?—I put some lettuces into the clock, and tried to wind up the rabbit!"

"Did the rabbit *go*, after you wound it up?" said Alice.

Humpty Dumpty clasped his hands on the top of his head, and groaned. "Go? I should think it *did* go! Why, it's *gone*! And wherever it's gone to—that's what I *ca'n't* find out! I've done my best—I've read all the article 'Rabbit' in the Dictionary—without success. It's the same with the Lion and the Unicorn," he said, turning the pages. "*Which* is the Lion and *which* is the Unicorn? It's *most* important not to get two such animals confused together. And one's very liable to do it in their cases—both having mouths, you know—"

As there was only one door out of the room, Alice presumed it was safe to use it.

She did so.

And immediately—to her surprise—she found herself falling through space. It felt like the Rabbit-Hole again.

The surrounding walls were covered with all kinds of objects. Some hanging on nails. Some carried on shelves. She passed a hall-clock and an (open) rabbit-hutch. She looked down and saw a falling rabbit. Was it the one Humpty Dumpty lost?

But the more she looked the more she saw it was wearing clothes and looked exactly like the White Rabbit she knew.

Then she landed with a start.

She was quickly on her feet, and saw the White Rabbit hurrying purposefully into the distance, glancing at his pocket-watch. He was carrying a very elegant walking-stick, and she wondered if it was one of those that belonged to Humpty Dumpty, for it seemed to make him walk very fast.

She had just begun to chase after him—for surely he must be going to the Queen of Hearts' Birthday Party himself, being the Queen's Herald—when the appearance of the Rabbit began to change—

His ears turned into a high top hat. His watch turned into a tea-cup. And his walking-stick into a tea-table.

CHAPTER III

"He Thought He Saw"

The White Rabbit had vanished, and she found herself walking instead towards a slightly over-grown garden, containing a very familiar *tableau*. There was a familiar empty armchair, just waiting for her to sit down in it.

Crossing a little brook, she rejoined the March Hare's Tea-Party. She remembered how she had left it long ago. In reply to one of their remarks, she had said "I don't think—" and before she could finish, the Hatter had said, "Then you shouldn't talk!" And of course she couldn't stay after *that*.

But it was as if Time had stood still since that moment, for she now heard the Hatter saying to her: "*We* think. That's why *we* talk." And rising from his chair, he began:—

"He thought he saw an Elephant,
*   That practised on a fife:*
He looked again, and found it was
*   A letter from his wife.*
'At length I realize,' he said,
*   'The bitterness of Life!'"*

He thought he saw a Buffalo
Upon the chimney-piece:
He looked again, and found it was
His Sister's Husband's Niece.
'Unless you leave this house,' he said,
'I'll send for the Police!'

"He thought he saw a Garden-Door
That opened with a key:
He looked again, and found it was
A Double Rule of Three:
'And all its mystery,' he said,
'Is clear as day to me!'"

He abruptly sat down, and the March Hare jumped up and continued:—

"He thought he saw a Banker's Clerk
    Descending from the bus:
He looked again, and found it was
    A Hippopotamus:
'If this should stay to dine,' he said,
    'There wo'n't be much for us!'"

"He thought he saw an Albatross
    That fluttered round the lamp:
He looked again, and found it was
    A Penny-Postage-Stamp.
'You'd best be getting home,' he said:
    'The nights are very damp!'"

> "He thought he saw a Rattlesnake
>   That questioned him in Greek:
> He looked again, and found it was
>   The Middle of Next Week.
> 'The one thing I regret,' he said,
>   'Is that it cannot speak!'"

The March Hare sat down.

There was a pause.

The lid of the teapot slowly lifted up, and the Dormouse raised his sleepy head and said:—

> "He thought he saw a Coach-and-Four
>   That stood beside his bed:
> He looked again, and found it was
>   A Bear without a Head.
> 'Poor thing,' he said, 'poor silly thing!
>   It's waiting to be fed!'"

"*He thought he saw a Kangaroo*
  That worked a coffee-mill:
He looked again, and found it was
  A Vegetable-Pill.
'*Were I to swallow this,*' *he said,*
  '*I should be very ill!*'"

"*He thought he saw an Argument*
  That proved he was the Pope:
He looked again, and found it was
  A Bar of Mottled Soap.
'*A fact so dread,*' *be faintly said,*
  '*Extinguishes all hope!*'"

As he finished the verse, the Hatter and Hare rushed forward and pushed the lid (a very elaborate one) back down on the teapot.

"Why did you stop him?" asked Alice.

The Hatter looked dismayed. "If you once let him begin *reciting*," he said, "he'll never leave off again!"

"Has it happened often?"

The March Hare dipped a pocket-watch into his tea and examined the dial. "Three times," he said.

"What became of the three poems?" Alice asked. "Is he saying them still?"

"Of course he is!"

This puzzled Alice so much she gave it up, saying instead: "Those are *very* curious verses. Can you explain them to me?"

"Choose one and I'll try," said the Hatter.

Alice thought for a moment, then began the first verse:—

"He thought he saw an Elephant
That practised on a—"

"I ca'n't explain that one," the Hatter interrupted. "It hasn't happened yet."

"It hasn't happened yet?" repeated Alice, unsure she understood.

"Yes. You are quite right. It hasn't. Some of the verses refer to things that *have* happened. The others, obviously, refer to things that haven't happened *yet*. It's very hard—almost impossible—to explain things that haven't happened. Don't you agree?"

Alice *did* agree.

"They all refer to someone somewhere," he added. "Sometimes to people who haven't been born yet. Ask another."

This didn't sound very promising, but Alice tried again:—

"He thought he saw a Buffalo
Upon the chimney-piece:
He looked again, and found it was
His Sister's Husband's Niece.
'Unless you leave this house,' he said,
'I'll send for the Police!'"

"That was *me*," the Hatter explained, looking at Alice across the tea-table. "And that's what I'd have done—called the Police—as sure as potatoes aren't radishes—if she hadn't taken herself off! I have so many half-brothers and half-sisters—"

"You shouldn't have so many *bits* of people lying around," interrupted the March Hare. "It's *very* untidy."

"And *you* talk too much. Do you think the world was *made* for you to talk in?"

"Why, where would you *have* me talk, then?" the March Hare said, evidently quite ready for an argument.

"I'm not going to discuss it now. It's too near tea-time."

"Get away with you! What does *that* signify?"

"I ca'n't get anywhere *without* myself. It's too difficult. I have so many half-brothers and half-sisters—" he paused, but the March Hare said nothing "—but I always love my *pay-rints* like anything!"

"Who *are* your *pay-rints?*" said Alice.

"Them as pay *rint* for me, of course!" the Hatter replied. "Now choose another!"

Alice thought again. Then said, "What about this:—

> *"He thought he saw an Albatross*
> *That fluttered round the lamp:*
> *He looked again, and found it was*
> *A Penny-Postage-Stamp.*
> *'You'd best be getting home,' he said:*
> *'The nights are very damp!'"*

"That was *me*," said the March Hare. "*I* spoke to the Postage-Stamp. *I* advised it to go home. *I* warned it about the damp."

"Would it be afraid of catching cold?" said Alice.

"If it got *very* damp, it might stick to something, you know. And *that* something would have to go by post, whatever it was! Suppose it was a cow! Wouldn't it be *dreadful* for the other things!"

"Pick another!" said the Hatter.

Alice considered. After some hesitation (they were getting harder to remember), she recalled:—

> *"He thought he saw a Garden-Door*
> *That opened with a key:*
> *He looked again, and found it was*
> *A Double Rule of Three:*
> *'And all its mystery,' he said,*
> *'Is clear as day to me!'"*

The Hatter smiled knowingly. "Why, that's *easy*! It's all about *you*!"

"Me?" said Alice.

"Yes! When you left us, didn't you open a door into the Garden of the Queen of Hearts? Where she was playing Croquet and threatening to cut off everyone's head? And didn't you use a golden key?

"Ye–e–s," admitted Alice reluctantly. "But, to begin with—it says *he*, and I'm not a *he*."

"Aren't you?"

"No! And what is 'A Double Rule of Three'?"

"A Double Rule of Three means you saw two groups of three rulers. The first group you saw was ourselves. *We* rule the tea-table. Then you saw the three gardeners. *They* rule the

Queen's Garden. When they explained why they were painting the roses red, the mystery became 'as clear as day'."

"And when you left *us*," interrupted the March Hare, "you said you would never return. Time doesn't like it when people say they'll never do a thing again. He always makes sure they do. That's why Time put you back to the exact point at which you left us. Now ask another!"

But Alice was still so disconcerted at the idea of the poem referring to herself—it had quite taken her breath away—that it took a little while to gather her thoughts, and by the time she had, she could only remember the very last verse:—

> *"He thought he saw an Argument*
> *That proved he was the Pope:*
> *He looked again, and found it was*
> *A Bar of Mottled Soap.*
> *'A fact so dread,' he faintly said,*
> *'Extinguishes all hope!'*

"What is *that* about?"

"That is all about *him*," said the Hatter, indicating the Dormouse, who had somehow extricated himself un-noticed from the teapot, and was now seated between the Hatter and the March Hare.

"Did *he* see the Bar of Mottled Soap?" Alice enquired.

"Oh, certainly!" said the Hatter. "That verse is the story of his life."

"He must have had a very curious life," said Alice.

"You may say that," said the Hatter.

"Of course she may!" cried the March Hare.

Alice saw tears of sympathy glitter in the March Hare's eyes. "I'm *very* sorry he isn't the Pope," he went on. "Aren't *you* sorry?"

"Well—I hardly know," Alice replied in the vaguest manner. "Would it make him any happier?"

"It wouldn't make the *Pope* any happier," said the Hatter.

"Oh!" Alice cried in sudden alarm. "Whatever is going to happen?"

For a number of trees, on the neighbouring hillside, were moving slowly upwards in solemn procession: while the mild little brook, that had been rippling at her feet a moment before, began to swell, and foam, and hiss, and bubble in a truly alarming fashion.

She heard the Hatter saying, as if through a closing door, "Look out for words in Greek. Look out for rattles. Look out for pills. Look out for stamps. But most of all—look out for Elephants!"

CHAPTER IV

The Gryphon
and the Mock Turtle

hen the landscape, which had been showing signs of mental aberration in various directions, settled down again—and Alice found the little brook had turned into a vast sea, and she was on the shore of it in the company of the Gryphon and the Mock Turtle. An easel, with a blackboard on it, stood a little way off, and the Gryphon held in his hand a piece of chalk. He was evidently giving the Mock Turtle lessons of some kind.

"You shouldn't be so lazy in the morning. Remember, it's the *early* bird that picks up the worm!"

"It may, if it likes!" the Mock Turtle said with a slight yawn. "I don't like eating worms one bit. I always stop in bed till the early bird has picked them up!"

"In the morning you should get up *at once*," said the Gryphon with an air of authority.

"Why *at once?*" said the Mock Turtle.

"Because you ca'n't get up at twice. It would hurt you to be divided."

"I don't *want* to be divided," said the Mock Turtle decisively.

"It does very well on a *diagram*," said the Gryphon. "I could show it you in a minute, only the chalk's a little blunt."

"Take care!" Alice anxiously exclaimed, as he began, rather clumsily, to sharpen the chalk. "You'll cut your finger off, if you hold the knife so!"

"If you cut it off, will you give it to *me*, please?" the Mock Turtle thoughtfully added.

"It's like this," said the Gryphon, hastily drawing a long line upon the blackboard, and marking the letters "A", "B", at the two ends, and "C" in the middle: "let me explain it to you. If AB were to be divided into two parts at C—"

"It would be drowned," the Mock Turtle pronounced confidently.

The Gryphon gasped. "*What* would be drowned?"

"Why the bumble-bee, of course!" said the Mock Turtle. "And the two bits would sink down in the sea!"

Here the Gryphon was evidently too much puzzled to go on with his diagram, and rubbed it out, using a sponge dipped in a rock-pool. "When I said being divided would *hurt* you, I was merely referring to the action of the nerves. The action of the nerves," he continued eagerly, "is curiously slow in some people. I had a friend once, that, if you burnt him with a red-hot poker, it would take years and years before he felt it!"

"And if you only *pinched* him?" queried Alice.

"Then it would take ever so much longer, of course. In fact, I doubt if the man *himself* would ever feel it, at all. His grandchildren might."

"I wouldn't like to be the grandchild of a pinched grandfather," said the Mock Turtle in a low voice. "It might come just when I wanted to be happy!"

"In your case, that would be *never*. Now really, we *must* get on with the Lessons," said the Gryphon impatiently.

"I hate it when you say 'really'. Why are *bad* things more real than good ones?"

"Eh? What are you talking about?"

"Whenever you say 'really' it always means there is something horrible coming!"

"That's because you always forget your Lessons!"

"I always remember *my* Lessons. It's other people's I find so hard to remember. I ca'n't think enough to remember them. They need *double* thinking, I believe."

"Double thinking? There's no such thing."

"There is. And double speaking. Whenever you say 'I must say *one* thing,' you always say at least *two*!"

"But I thought all his lessons were ended," objected Alice. "They got 'less and less', you know."

"Only his lessons under the sea. When *they* ended his lessons on land began. He belongs to sea *and* land. When the sea grows less the land grows more."

"So when the sea grows more again—"

"His lessons under the sea grow more again."

"I *ca'n't* learn any more!" cried the Mock Turtle.

"What?! I wonder you have the face to say such a thing."

"I don't need a face to say it. Just a mouth."

"What I mean is, you know you can if you like."

"Of course I can, if I *like*," the pale student replied; "But I ca'n't if I *don't* like!"

"There's only three lessons to do," said the Gryphon. "No Arithmetic, and Spelling, and Singing."

"No Arithmetic?" said Alice.

"No, he hasn't a head for Arithmetic—"

"Of course I haven't," said the Mock Turtle. "My head's for *hair*. I haven't got a *lot* of heads!"

"—and he ca'n't repeat his Multiplication Table—"

"I like *history* ever so much better," the Mock Turtle remarked. "You have to *repeat* the Multiplication Table. But History repeats *itself*."

The Gryphon wrote some letters on the board. "Now, what does *that* spell?"

The Mock Turtle looked at it, in solemn silence, for a minute. "I know what it *doesn't* spell!" he said at last.

"That's *quite* enough of Spelling," said the Gryphon. "We'll do some more another time. Now we shall sing the Song of the Three Badgers." He turned over the blackboard, and there were the words all set out. And this is how they sang it:—

Gryphon:
> *"There be three Badgers on a mossy stone*
> *Beside a dark and covered way:*
> *Each dreams himself a monarch on his throne,*
> *And so they stay and stay—*
> *Though their old Father languishes alone,*
> *They stay, and stay, and stay."*

Mock Turtle:

> *"There be three Herrings loitering around,*
> > *Longing to share that mossy seat:*
> *Each Herring tries to sing what she has found*
> > *That makes Life seem so sweet.*
> *Thus with a grating and uncertain sound,*
> > *They bleat, and bleat, and bleat."*

(The Mock Turtle was very good at bleating.)

Alice:

> *"Oh, dear beyond our dearest dreams*
> > *Fairer than all that fairest seems*
> *To feast the rosy hours away,*
> *To revel in a roundelay!*
> > *How blest would be*
> > *A life so free—*
> *Ipwergis-Pudding to consume,*
> *And drink the subtle Azzigoom!"*

Gryphon:

> *"The Mother-Herring on the salt sea-wave,*
> *Sought vainly for her absent ones:*
> *The Father-Badger, writhing in a cave,*
> *Shrieked out 'Return, my sons!*
> *You shall have buns,' he shrieked, 'if you'll behave!*
> *Yea, buns, and buns, and buns!'"*

Mock Turtle:

> *"'I fear,' said she, 'your sons have gone astray?*
> *My daughters left me while I slept.'*
> *'Yes'm,' the Badger said: 'it's as you say.*
> *They should be better kept.'*
> *Thus the poor parents talked the time away,*
> *And wept, and wept, and wept."*

(The Mock Turtle was very good at weeping).

Alice:

> *"Oh, dear beyond our dearest dreams*
> > *Fairer than all that fairest seems*
> *To feast the rosy hours away,*
> *To revel in a roundelay!*
> > *How blest would be*
> > *A life so free—*
> *Ipwergis-Pudding to consume,*
> *And drink the subtle Azzigoom!"*

Gryphon and Mock Turtle:

> *"The Badgers did not care to talk to Fish:*
> > *They did not dote on Herrings' songs:*
> *They never had experienced the dish*
> > *To which that name belongs:*
> *'And oh, to pinch their tails,' (this was their wish),*
> > *'With tongs, yea, tongs, and tongs!'*
>
> *"'And are not these the Fish,' the Eldest sighed,*
> > *'Whose Mother dwells beneath the foam?'*
> *'They ARE the fish!' the Second one replied.*
> > *'And they have left their home!'*
> *'Oh wicked Fish,' the youngest Badger cried,*
> > *'To roam, yea, roam, and roam! '*
>
> *"Gently the Badgers trotted to the shore—*
> > *The sandy shore that fringed the bay:*
> *Each in his mouth a living Herring bore—*
> > *Those aged ones waxed gay:*
> *Clear rang their voices through the ocean's roar,*
> > *'Hooray, hooray, hooray!'"*

(The Gryphon and Mock Turtle danced wildly in celebration.)

Gryphon and Mock Turtle and Alice (final chorus):
> *"And if, in other days and hours*
> *Mid other fluffs and other flowers,*
> *The choice were given me how to dine*
> *'Name what thou wilt: it shall be thine!'*
> *Oh, then I see*
> *The life for me*
> *Ipwergis-Pudding to consume,*
> *And drink the subtle Azzigoom!"*

"So they all got safe home again," the Mock Turtle said, after waiting a minute to see if Alice had anything more to say: he evidently felt that *some* remark ought to be made.

The Gryphon considered a little, before giving his verdict on the Mock Turtle's performance.

"Well," he said at last, "some of the notes are the same as others—and some are different—but I should hardly call it a *tune*."

"Never mind what you *should* call it. What *do* you call it?"

"For the sake of argument, let us assume that it began on *A flat*."

"I can usually manage very well *on the flat*."

"It didn't *sound* like *A flat*."

"What *did* it sound like?"

"It sounded more like *a duck*."

"Single notes are apt to have that effect," said the Mock Turtle with a sigh.

"How do *you* like his singing?" the Gryphon asked Alice in a low voice.

"He bleats well," said Alice, a little evasively. "And he weeps well—"

"But how do you like his *singing*?" insisted the Gryphon.

"It isn't very *beautiful*," Alice said, hesitatingly.

"It's extremely *ugly*!" the Gryphon said, without any hesitation at all.

But the Gryphon's words reached Alice very faintly, for suddenly a loud wind was blowing in from the sea. The figures of the Gryphon and the Mock Turtle became vague and shadowy, while the beach—was it its turn to 'grow less'?—was retreating rapidly from her sight.

"Oh dear!" said Alice. "Things change so, here. Whenever I look again, it's bound to be something different!

"Good-bye!" she cried to the Gryphon and Mock Turtle: but their voices sounded strange and far away, and they took not the slightest notice of her farewell.

The scene abruptly changed.

She was now in the heart of a quiet wood.

She looked in vain for her companions. They had vanished with the storm, and there was nothing for it but to make the best of her way alone.

The wind was slowly dropping, and blew more and more gently as she walked into it, till she could see where it began.

It was caused—though how such a small thing could have so great an effect totally puzzled her—by nothing more than a butterfly fluttering its wings as it sat on the branch of a tree.

Its body and legs were the body and legs of a hookah, and the tubes of the hookah formed its wings.

This made Alice quite certain it had formerly been the blue Caterpillar.

He wore a spotted kerchief round his head, such as old people wore to keep warm in bed, and his two antennae were covered by a bow.

"Oh, Sir! Please stop for a moment!" cried Alice, for though her memories of the Caterpillar were not entirely pleasant, she would have liked to renew her acquaintance with it. "Don't you remember me? We met when you were a caterpillar."

He puffed on the mouthpiece of the hookah, as if to jog his memory; then, after an interval, in a voice just as languid as Alice remembered it, said,

"I've been to sleep since then."

Alice supposed its sleep in the chrysalis *must* have been a very deep one. Perhaps he didn't remember *anyone* it met during its time as a caterpillar.

"Do *you* sleep much?" said the Butterfly.

"Not to excess, I think," said Alice, rather proudly.

"Ah," said the Butterfly. "To be a really good example, you shouldn't sleep at all."

Alice ventured to believe that this was an example too lofty for her to attain, no matter how hard she tried.

"After you've borrowed money," he said, "do you pay it back?"

"Of course."

"To be a really good example, you should pay the money back *before* you borrow it."

"But that's impossible!"

"Not at all. Have you never heard of robbing Peter to pay Paul?

> *'Peter is poor,' said noble Paul,*
> *   'And I have always been his friend:*
> *And, though my means to GIVE are small,*
> *   At least I can afford to lend.*
> *How few, in this cold age of greed,*
> *   Do good, except on selfish grounds!*
> *But I can feel for Peter's need,*
> *   And I WILL LEND HIM FIFTY POUNDS!'*

How great was Peter's joy to find
  His friend in such a genial vein!
How cheerfully the bond he signed,
  To pay the money back again!
'We ca'n't,' said Paul, 'be too precise:
  'Tis best we fix the very day:
So, by a learned friend's advice,
  I've made it Noon, the Fourth of May.'

'But this is April!' Peter said.
  'The First of April, as I think.
Five little weeks will soon be fled:
  One scarcely will have time to wink!
Give me a year to speculate—
  To buy and sell—to drive a trade—'
Said Paul 'I cannot change the date.
  On May the Fourth it must be paid.'

'Well, well!' said Peter, with a sigh.
　　'Hand me the cash, and I will go.
I'll form a Joint-Stock company,
　　And turn an honest pound or so.'
'I'm grieved', said Paul, 'to seem unkind:
　　The money shall of course be lent:
But, for a week or two, I find
　　It will not be convenient.'

So, week by week, poor Peter came
　　And turned in heaviness away;
For still the answer was the same,
　　'I cannot manage it to-day.'
And now the April showers were dry
　　The five short weeks were nearly spent
Yet still he got the old reply,
　　'It is not quite convenient!'

The Fourth arrived, and punctual Paul
 Came, with his legal friend, at noon.
'I thought it best', said he, 'to call:
 One cannot settle things too soon.'
Poor Peter shuddered in despair:
 His flowing locks he wildly tore:
And very soon his yellow hair
 Was lying all about the floor.

The legal friend was standing by,
 With sudden pity half unmanned:
The tear-drop trembled in his eye,
 The signed agreement in his hand:
But when at length the legal soul
 Resumed its customary force,
'The Law', he said, 'we ca'n't control:
 Pay, or the Law must take its course!'

Said Paul 'How bitterly I rue
 That fatal morning when I called!
Consider, Peter, what you do!
 You wo'n't be richer when you're bald!
Think you, by rending curls away
 To make your difficulties less?
Forbear this violence, I pray:
 You do but add to my distress!'

'Not willingly would I inflict',
 Said Peter, 'on that noble heart
One needless pang. Yet why so strict?
 Is THIS *to act a friendly part?*
However legal it may be
 To pay what never has been lent,
This style of business seems to me
 Extremely inconvenient!'

"So you'll see in a moment how perfectly possible it is. Though it does have *some* inconveniences," he admitted.

"What a *horrid* man Paul was!" said Alice indignantly. "Making poor Peter pay back what he hadn't even borrowed yet!"

"He didn't charge him interest. He could have, you know."

Alice wasn't sure what to say to this. So she resumed a more pleasant subject. "Do you remember me now? You told me to eat some of a mushroom if I wanted to change my size."

He puffed on the hookah again, then after his customary pause, said, "Well? You changed it didn't you?"

Alice couldn't deny she *was* rather larger than her previous three inches.

"Yes, but can you please show me the way to the Queen of Hearts' Birthday Party?"

"Are you happy with the size you are now?"

"Yes."

"Then ask someone your own size."

"*Who?*" begged Alice.

The cloud of smoke became greater, and through it, to her amazement, Alice saw the Butterfly get bigger. He grew bigger and bigger till he *was* Alice's own size. But his size *and* appearance had changed, and when the smoke cleared, instead of an insect sitting on a branch, she saw a man sitting on a horse, travelling very slowly along a path between the trees.

CHAPTER V

The Knight is Old

"Oh, White Knight! How wonderful to see you again! Can you please show me the way to the Queen of Hearts' Birthday Party?"

"Of course, my dear," he replied in the gentle tones she knew so well. "I'm going there myself. Would you like to accompany me?"

Alice was only too glad to do so—despite the fact he *still* kept falling off his horse.

At last he commented, "I'm working on an invention, to do without the trouble of having a horse to carry me. My invention is—for carrying one's *self*, you know. It wants just a *little* more working out."

"Wo'n't that be very tiring, to carry *yourself*?" Alice enquired.

"Well, no, my child. You see, whatever fatigue one incurs by *carrying*, one saves by *being carried*!"

Alice noticed that from his saddle hung a pair of very strange-looking boots, the tops of which were open umbrellas.

"I thought you'd like to see them," said the White Knight with a smile, noticing the direction of Alice's gaze. "These are the boots for horizontal weather!"

"But what's the use of wearing umbrellas round one's knees?"

"In *ordinary* rain," the White Knight admitted, "they would *not* be of much use. But if ever the Barometer moved, not up and down, but *sideways*, and brought *horizontal* rain, they would be invaluable—simply invaluable.

"I've been suffering," he added, "from lumbago and rheumatism, and that kind of thing. But I've been curing *myself*. Why, I've actually invented three new diseases, besides a new way of breaking my collar-bone!"

"Is it a nice way?" said Alice.

"Well, hum, not *very*," the White Knight admitted.

"One of my inventions," he continued, "is to run railway-trains without any engines—nothing is needed but machinery to stop them with."

"But where does the *force* come from?" Alice ventured to ask.

"They use the force of gravity."

"But that would need a railway always going *down-hill*," Alice remarked. "You ca'n't have *all* your railways going down-hill?"

"I can," said the White Knight simply.

"From both ends?"

"From *both* ends."

"Can you explain the process?" asked Alice. "That is, without using difficult words?"

"Easily. Each railway is in a long tunnel, perfectly straight: so of course the *middle* of it is nearer the centre of the globe than the two ends are, so every train runs half-way *down*-hill, and that gives it force enough to run the *other* half *up*-hill."

"I see!" said Alice. "That explains it beautifully."

"Another of my inventions is to stop runaway horses. Would you like to hear it?"

"Very much!"

"At present, a runaway horse is a very real danger. That is because the carriage is wholly *behind* the horse. The horse runs. The carriage follows. The horse has the bit between his teeth. Who shall stop him? He flies faster and faster. Finally comes the inevitable upset. But my invention would prevent all that! Our horse is harnessed in the very centre of our carriage. Two wheels are in front of him, and two behind. To the roof is attached one end of a broad belt. This goes under the horse's body, and the other end is attached to a little windlass. The horse takes the bit in his teeth. He runs away. We are flying at ten miles an hour! We turn our little windlass, five turns, six turns, seven turns, and—poof! Our horse is off the ground! *Now* let him gallop in the air as much as he pleases: our *carriage* stands still. We sit round him, and watch him till he is tired. Then we let him down. Our horse is glad, very much glad, when his feet once more touch the ground."

Alice wondered whether it was *entirely* practical, but did not voice her misgivings.

By now he had managed such a long period of staying in his saddle, that it quite cheered him up, and he began to sing:—

> *"King Fisher courted Lady Bird—*
> *SING BEANS, SING BONES, SING BUTTERFLIES!*
> *'Find me my match,' he said,*
> *'With such a noble head—*
> *With such a beard, as white as curd—*
> *With such expressive eyes!'*

"'Yet pins have heads,' said Lady Bird—
SING PRUNES, SING PRAWNS, SING PRIMROSE-HILL!
    'And where you stick them in,
    They stay, and thus a pin
Is very much to be preferred
    To one that's never still!'

"'Oysters have beards,' said Lady Bird—
SING FLIES, SING FROGS, SING FIDDLE-STRINGS!
    'I love them, for I know
    THEY never chatter so:
They would not say one single word
    Not if you crowned them Kings!'

> *"'Needles have eyes,' said Lady Bird—*
> *SING CATS, SING CORKS, SING COWSLIP-TEA!*
> *'And they are sharp—just what*
> *Your Majesty is NOT:*
> *So get you gone—'tis too absurd*
> *To come a-courting me!'"*

As he finished the song, he fell off his horse. It was a particularly heavy fall.

As Alice bent to help the White Knight up, she heard a voice say: "May I help you?"

Looking round she saw a boy with long hair, dressed in a medieval tunic, and carrying a sword. She had seen him before. But where? Then she remembered. In the book in Looking-Glass Land. It was the Boy who had slain the Jabberwock.

"Yes, please," said Alice.

The White Knight lay as if he would never move again.

"Don't you pity his grey hairs?" said Alice.

"I pity his *self*. But I don't pity his *hair* one bit. His *hair* ca'n't feel!"

Alice and the Boy managed to get him sitting up.

"You should go for a stay at the seaside," Alice said tenderly. "It'd do you ever so much good! And the Sea's so grand!"

"But a Mountain's grander!!' said the Boy, helping the White Knight to his feet.

"What is there grand about a Mountain?" said the White Knight, as they put his left foot into its stirrup. "When you're bigger, mountains wo'n't look so grand. The grandeur of a mountain depends on its size relative to ours. Double the height of the mountain, and of course it's twice as grand. Halve my height, and you produce the same effect. Happy, happy, happy Small! None but the Short, none but the Short, none but the Short enjoy the Tall!

"And what is there grand about the Sea?" he went on, turning to Alice. "Why, you could put it all into a teacup!"

"*Some* of it," Alice corrected, assisting the Boy in pushing the White Knight further onto his horse.

"Well, you'd only want a certain number of tea-cups to hold it *all*. And *then* where's the grandeur? It's the same with a Mountain—why, you could carry it all away in a wheel-barrow, in a certain number of years!" (The White Knight was almost in his saddle by now.)

"It wouldn't look grand—the bits of it in the wheel-barrow," Alice candidly admitted.

"But when you put it together again——" the Boy began.

"When you're older," said the White Knight, "you'll know that you ca'n't put Mountains together again so easily! One lives and one learns, you know!"

"But it needn't be the *same* one, need it?" said the Boy. "Wo'n't it do, if I live, and some one *else* learns?"

"I *ca'n't* learn without living," said Alice.

"But I *can* live without learning!" the Boy retorted. "You just try me!" (He managed to get the White Knight's *right* foot into its stirrup.)

"What I meant, was—" the White Knight began, looking much puzzled, "—was—that you don't know *everything*, you know."

"But I *do* know everything I know!" persisted the little fellow. "I know ever so many things! Everything, except the things I *don't* know. And someone else knows all the rest."

The White Knight sighed and gave it up. "What a singular boy you are!" be whispered to himself: but the Boy had caught the words.

"I'm very glad I *am* a singular boy! It would be *horrid* to be two or three boys! Perhaps they wouldn't play with me!"

CHAPTER VI

The Knight is Young

The White Knight was now ready to proceed on his horse, and the Boy happily added himself to their number as they journied to the Party.

"How far have you come?" asked the Boy.

The White Knight looked uncertain. "A mile or two, I *think*," he said doubtfully.

"I've come a mile or *three*," said the Boy.

"You shouldn't say 'a mile or *three*'," the White Knight corrected him.

Alice nodded approval. "I quite agree. It isn't usual to say 'a mile or *three*'."

"It would be usual—if we said it often enough," said the Boy.

"He's very quick for his age!" the White Knight murmured. "You're not more than Seven, are you?" he added aloud.

"I'm not so many as *that*," said the Boy. "I'm *one*. You're *one*. She's *one*. One and One and One is Three."

"Oh, I wasn't *counting* you, you know!" he replied.

"Haven't you *learnt* to count?" said the Boy.

"When I asked if you were *seven*, I was merely commenting on the smallness of your stature."

"I know a song about someone like that," said the Boy eagerly. "Listen!" And as he walked along he began to sing:—

"In Stature the Manlet was dwarfish
　No burly big Blunderbore he:
And he wearily gazed on the crawfish
　His Wifelet had dressed for his tea.
'Now reach me, sweet Atom, my gunlet,
　And hurl the old shoelet for luck:
Let me hie to the bank of the runlet,
　　　　　And shoot thee a Duck!'

"She has reached him his minikin gunlet:
　She has hurled the old shoelet for luck:
She is busily baking a bunlet,
　To welcome him home with his Duck.
On he speeds, never wasting a wordlet,
　Though thoughtlets cling, closely as wax,
To the spot where the beautiful birdlet
　　　　　So quietly quacks."

Where the Lobsterlet lurks, and the Crablet
  So slowly and sleepily crawls:
Where the Dolphin's at home, and the Dablet
  Pays long ceremonious calls:
Where the Grublet is sought by the Froglet:
  Where the Frog is pursued by the Duck:
Where the Ducklet is chased by the Doglet—
    So runs the world's luck!

He has loaded with bullet and powder:
  His footfall is noiseless as air:
But the Voices grow louder and louder,
  And bellow, and bluster, and blare.
They bristle before him and after,
  They flutter above and below,
Shrill shriekings of lubberly laughter,
    Weird wailings of woe!

They echo without him, within him:
    They thrill through his whiskers and beard:
Like a teetotum seeming to spin him,
    With sneers never hitherto sneered.
'Avengement,' they cry, 'on our Foelet!
    Let the Manikin weep for our wrongs!
Let us drench him, from toplet to toelet,
                With Nursery-Songs!

'He shall muse upon "Hey! Diddle! Diddle!"
    On the Cow that surmounted the Moon:
He shall rave of the Cat aind the Fiddle,
    And the Dish that eloped with the Spoon:
And his soul shall be sad for the Spider,
    When Miss Muffet was sipping her whey,
That so tenderly sat down beside her,
                And scared her away!

'The music of Midsummer-madness
        Shall sting him with many a bite,
Till, in rapture of rollicking sadness,
        He shall groan with a gloomy delight:
He shall swathe him, like mists of the morning,
        In platitudes luscious and limp,
Such as deck, with a deathless adorning,
                The Song of the Shrimp!

'When the Ducklet's dark doom is decided,
        We will trundle him home in a trice:
And the banquet, so plainly provided,
        Shall round into rose-buds and rice:
In a blaze of pragmatic invention
        He shall wrestle with Fate, and shall reign:
But he has not a friend fit to mention,
                So hit him again!"

He has shot it, the delicate darling!
And the Voices have ceased from their strife:
Not a whisper of sneering or snarling,
As he carries it home to his wife:
Then, cheerily champing the bunlet
His spouse was so skilful to bake,
He hies him once more to the runlet,
To fetch her the Drake!

As he finished his song, they emerged from the Wood.

The path took them to a little rising ground, and when they mounted it they gained a view of the whole land at once. In the background were mountains, and in the foreground gleamed the dome of a white Pavilion, nestled in a park, and surrounded by many attractive walkways, with people going up and down them. The Boy stopped with his hands clasped together. At last he drew a long breath, and gave his verdict— in a hurried whisper, and without the slightest regards to grammar: "It's the loveliest thing as I never saw in all my life before!"

The White Knight dismounted, and gathering into his arms some of the items the horse had carried, murmured softly: "Happy, happy, happy Small! None but the Short, none but the Short, none but the Short enjoy the Tall!"

"What are you taking to give the Queen of Hearts for her Birthday?" Alice asked him.

"A Lecture."

"Oh!" said Alice. (She was very glad she didn't get that kind of present for *her* birthday, and she seriously doubted how well it would be received by her Majesty.)

"It *has* taken me a goodish time to prepare. I've got so many other things to attend to. For instance, I'm Court-Physician. I have to keep all the Royal Servants in good health—and that reminds me!" he cried, as they approached the large wooden door. "This is Medicine-Day! We only give Medicine once a week. If we were to begin giving it every day, the bottles would *soon* be empty!" He hurriedly rang the bell.

"But if they were ill on the *other* days?" Alice suggested.

"What, ill on the wrong *day?*" exclaimed the White Knight. "Oh, that would never do! A servant would be dismissed *at once*, who was ill on the wrong day! This is the Medicine for *today*," he went on, taking a large bottle out of a bag. "I mixed it, myself, first thing this morning."

"What is the Medicine *made* of?" said Alice.

The White Knight's answer was anything but encouraging. "Bits of things!" He held out the bottle. "Taste it!" he said. "Dip in your finger and taste it!"

Alice, who had grown rather cautious about what she ate and drank in Wonderland, declined, but the Boy accepted the Medicine, and made such an excruciatingly wry face that Alice was very glad she had *not* made the experiment.

"It's extremely nasty!" the Boy said, as his face resumed its natural shape.

"Nasty?" said the White Knight. "Why, of *course* it is! What would Medicine be, if it wasn't *nasty?*"

"Nice," said the Boy.

"I was going to say—" the White Knight faltered rather taken aback by the promptness of the Boy's reply, "—-that *that* would never do! Medicine *has* to be nasty, you know. The *medicine's* the great thing; the *diseases* are much less important. You can keep a medicine for years and years: but nobody ever wants to keep a Disease! Allow me to offer you a vegetable-pill also."

"Would it taste worse than the bottle of Medicine?"

"*Much* worse," said the White Knight proudly.

"Then I'd rather not, thank you. I'm afraid it would make me very ill.

"I wouldn't like to keep a Disease," said the Boy, turning to Alice. "But I like keeping Birthdays. I keep them on the second shelf of my cupboard."

"What do you keep on the other shelves?" asked Alice.

"Promises. You have to put *salt* with them, of course," he added gravely. "You ca'n't keep promises without any salt."

"But how long does a birthday *keep*? I never can keep *mine* for more than twenty-four hours."

"Why, a birthday stays *that* long just by itself," cried the Boy. "You don't know how to keep birthdays! I keep mine for *ever so much longer* than that!"

Suddenly a voice came from a window beside the door. "*You mustn't come in before the doors are opened!*"

"We *ca'n't*," said the White Knight.

Then, immediately, the door *was* opened.

Alice saw that the voice belonged to the Fish-Footman. A creature she had once seen delivering an invitation to play croquet from the Queen of Hearts to the Duchess.

He evidently knew the White Knight. But he looked at the two children and said: "Give me your names!"

"We'd rather not!" the Boy exclaimed, pulling Alice away from the door. "We want them for ourselves!"

"Nonsense!" said Alice very decidedly. "My name is Alice, and this is—is—-the Boy who slew the Jabberwock!"

The Fish-Footman looked at the Boy.

"Any other Name?

"Of course! The Boy who slew the Jabberwock. *Esquire!*"

"Duke of Anything?" the Fish-Footman asked.

"Not Duke at all," replied the Boy, evidently a little ashamed to confess it.

"I suppose you're Sir Something, then?"

"No," he said, looking more and more ashamed. "I haven't got any title."

The Fish-Footman seemed to think that in that case he really wasn't worth talking to.

"You may both wait at table. You'd like that, wouldn't you? To hand about plates, and so on. I know one of the head-waiters. I could speak to him on your behalf."

"Well, but that's not the most *enjoyable* way of attending a Banquet, is it?" said Alice.

The Fish-Footman tossed his head, and said, in a rather offended tone, that they might do as they pleased—there were many he knew who would give their ears to do it.

"They invited me once, last week," the Fish-Footman added, very proudly. "It was to wash up the soup-plates—no, the cheese-plates I mean—that was grand enough. And I waited at table. And I didn't hardly make only *one* mistake. Which was bringing scissors to cut the beef with. But the grandest thing of all was, I fetched the King of Hearts a glass of cider!"

"That *was* grand!" admitted the Boy. "But that's not so nice as sitting at the table, is it?"

"Of course it isn't," the Fish-Footman said, in a tone as if he rather pitied his ignorance; "but if you're not even Sir Anything, you ca'n't expect to be allowed to sit at the table, you know."

"But look here, dear White Knight!" whispered Alice. "He needn't open the door for *us* at all. We can go in with *you*."

"True, dear child!" the White Knight thankfully replied. And after a great deal of looking among the things he carried, he produced a large envelope. "Here is my invitation," he said to the Fish-Footman. "These children are with *me*, and I *am* Sir Somebody, you know."

"You're big enough to be *two* Sir Somebodies," said the little creature as, without further objection, he let them in.

The White Knight said: "Be good enough to take this bottle down into the Servants' Hall, and tell them it's their Medicine for *today*."

"Which of them is to drink it?" the Fish-Footman asked, as he carried off the bottle, struggling so much as he gripped it that Alice couldn't help laughing.

"Oh, I've not settled *that* yet!" the White Knight briskly replied. "I'll come and settle that, later. Tell them not to begin, on any account, till I come. It's really *wonderful*," he said, turning to the children, "the success I've had curing Diseases! Here are some of my memoranda."

He produced a heap of little bits of paper, pinned together in twos and threes. "Just look at *this* set, now. 'Gave Under-Cook Number Thirteen a Double Dose of Medicine.' And now see what's pinned on top. 'Under-Cook Number Thirteen suffering from Common Fever—*Febris communis*.' And on top of *that*, 'Under-Cook Number Thirteen fully recovered!' *that's* something to be proud of, *isn't it?*"

"But which happened *first*?" said Alice, looking very much confused. "The Medicine or the Disease?"

The White Knight examined the papers carefully. "They are not *dated*, I find," he said with a slightly dejected air: "so I fear I ca'n't tell you. But they *both* happened: there's no doubt of *that*."

"Wonderful!" murmured Alice, surveying the mass of papers. "It's almost beyond belief!"

The White Knight took it as a compliment, and bowed with a gratified smile.

"*Quite* beyond belief!" the Boy added (meaning, no doubt, to be more complimentary still).

The White Knight bowed, but he didn't smile *this* time.

The Lecture is Introduced

The loud blast of a trumpet interrupted them. "Why, the entertainment has *begun*!" the White Knight exclaimed, as he hurried the children into the Banqueting Hall. "I had no idea it was so late!"

A small table, containing cake and wine, stood in the centre of the room; and here Alice found the King and Queen of Hearts waiting for them. Alice was much struck by the great change that had taken place in the faces of the Imperial Pair since she had last seen them. Still wearing a judge's wig under his crown, as if he'd forgotten to take it off, a vacant stare was now the *King's* usual expression; while over the face of the *Queen* there flitted, ever and anon, a grim smile.

The Queen of Hearts was a vast creature at all times; but, when she frowned and folded her arms, as now, she looked more gigantic than ever, and made one try to fancy what a haystack would look like, if out of temper.

"So you're come at last!" the Queen sulkily remarked, as the White Knight and the children approached the dining-tables.

Alice passed tables and chairs occupied by the King, Knave, and Queen of Spades, the King, Knave, and Queen of Clubs, and the King, Knave, and Queen of Diamonds. As she went by she remembered the nursery rhymes that referred to them, and heard a little of what they were saying.

> *The King of Spades,*
> *He kissed the maids,*
> *Which vexed the Queen full sore.*
> *The Queen of Spades*
> *She beat those maids,*
> *And turned them out of door.*

"For fifteen years," said the Queen of Spades in a harsh voice, "my husband has been the Sub-Excellency. It is too long! It is much too long! He would distinguish himself as a *Vice*-Excellency," she proceeded. "There has never been such a Vice as he would be! When my husband is Vice, it will be as if we had a hundred Vices!"

> *The King of Clubs*
> *He often drubs*
> *His loving Queen and wife;*
> *The Queen of Clubs*
> *Returns him snubs,*
> *And all is noise and strife.*

"What did you get this dagger for?" said the King of Clubs to his wife. "And made of tin, too!" he added scornfully, bending the blade round his thumb. "Come, no evasions! You ca'n't deceive *me*!"

"I got it for—for—for—" the Queen stammered. "For—"

"For *what*, Madam!"

"Well, for eighteen pence, if you *must* know! That's what I got it for, on my——-"

"Now *don't* say your Word and Honour!" he groaned. "Why, they aren't worth half the money, put together!"

"On my *Birthday*," the Queen concluded in a meek whisper.

> *The Diamond King*
> *I fain would sing*
> *And likewise his fair Queen,*
> *But that the Knave,*
> *A naughty slave,*
> *Must needs step in between.*

"I shall come to the Fancy-dress Ball," said the Queen of Diamonds to the Knave, "as a Dancing-Bear, and my husband shall be dressed as a Court-Jester, my Keeper. He looks, oh, such a *perfect* Fool! I'll have to practise the steps a bit.

"One ca'n't help being rather human, just at first, you know. And I sha'n't wear the Head *all* the time. It presents such difficulties when eating. What shall *you* come as?"

"I shall come as—as early as I can!"

It was evident that her Exalted Highness the Queen of Hearts (this was one of the Queen's many titles) was *very* much out of temper: and they were not long in learning the cause of this, for their companions at the dining-table began informing them of it in a series of whispers when they had taken their places.

"The King went to a window in the Queen's apartments—"

"—and remarked—"

"'My dear, is that the three gardeners I see down below, going about your flower beds?'"

"'They seem to be watering—"

"'—your roses—"

"'—with empty watering-cans.'"

"'*Empty* watering-cans!' shrieked her Majesty—"

"—rushing madly to the window—"

"—and almost pushing her husband out—"

"—in her anxiety to see for herself."

"Putting spectacles hastily on her nose—"

"—she *did* see for herself."

"The Queen stamped—"

"—which was undignified—"

"—and snorted—"

"—which was ungraceful."

"'What is the *meaning* of this?' she bellowed."

"The gardeners replied that it made them lighter to hold—putting a lot of water in them made their arms ache!"

Nor was this the only reason for her ill-temper. She did not consider the preparations, made for the Imperial Party, to be such as suited their rank. "A common mahogany table!" she growled, pointing to it contemptuously with her thumb. "Why wasn't it made of gold, I should like to know?"

"It would have taken a very long—" a servant began, but the Queen cut the sentence short.

"Then the cake! Ordinary plum! Why wasn't it made of—of—" She broke off again. "Then the wine! Merely old Madeira! Why wasn't it— Then this chair! That's worst of all. Why wasn't it a throne? One *might* excuse the other omissions, but I *ca'n't* get over the chair!"

"What *I* ca'n't get over," said the King, in eager sympathy with his wife, "is the *table*!"

"Pooh!" said the Queen, and marched out of the room, only remarking that she had some executions to arrange.

"It is much to be regretted!" the White Knight mildly replied, as soon as he had a chance of speaking. After a moment's thought he strengthened the remark. "*Everything,*" he said addressing Society in general, "is *very much* to be regretted!"

A murmur of "Hear, hear!" rose from the crowded Hall.

The Banqueting Hall was an eight-sided room, having in each angle a slender pillar, round which silken draperies were twined. The doorways between the pillars were entirely surrounded, to the height of six or seven feet, with creepers, from which hung quantities of ripe fruit and brilliant flowers, that almost hid the leaves. In another place, perchance, Alice might have wondered to see fruit and flowers growing together; here, her chief wonder was that neither fruit nor flowers were such as she had ever seen before. Higher up, each wall contained a circular window of coloured glass; and over all was an arched roof, that seemed to be spangled all over with jewels.

Alice sat at the mid-point of a long table, with the White Knight facing her, and the Boy who slew the Jabberwock on his right. Seeing their faces side by side—one in the Spring of life, one in the late Autumn—Alice noticed for the first time how curiously alike they were. When she called attention to this fact, the White Knight exclaimed,

"Of course we are! We're from Looking-glass Land. He is the younger reflection of me, and I am the older reflection of him."

A sentence that *sounded* well, but Alice couldn't quite understand it.

"May I go and eat one of those fruits?" said the Boy to the White Knight, gazing longingly at the fruit-laden creepers.

"Yes, child," said the White Knight sadly: "and then you'll find out what *pleasure* is like—the pleasure we all seek so madly, and enjoy so bitterly."

The Boy ran to the nearest creeper-covered wall, and picked a fruit that was *shaped* something like a banana., but had the *colour* of a strawberry.

He ate it with beaming looks, that became gradually more gloomy, and were very blank indeed by the time he had finished.

"It hasn't got any taste at all!" he complained. "I couldn't feel anything in my mouth! What *is* it?"

The White Knight gave his answer with a mournful smile. "It is called *dreamfruit*. One day you will discover that most things are like that—"

But the Boy didn't seem convinced, only puzzled. "I'll try *another* kind of fruit!" he said. "There's some lovely striped ones over there, just like a rainbow!" And off he ran.

He was soon picking and eating fruit from different creepers, in the vain hope of finding *some* that had a taste. He finally gave up on the attempt and returned to his seat.

"I've brought you these," he said shyly to Alice, and gave her a small bunch of flowers he'd gathered.

"Thank you," said Alice, "they're *very* pretty!" And she rewarded the Boy with a kiss.

She asked the White Knight for help in identifying them.

"*These* are all found in Central India!" he said, laying aside part of the bouquet. "They are rare, even there: and I have never seen them in any other part of the world. *These* two are Mexican—*this* one—I am nearly sure—" He held it to the light of a lamp. "Yes! This is the flower of the Upas-tree, which usually grows only in the depths of Indian forests; and the flower fades so quickly after being plucked, that it is scarcely possible to keep its form or colour even so far as the outskirts of the forest! Yet this is in full bloom!"

But even as he was speaking, a mysterious thing was happening to the flowers. They were melting entirely away!

"Oh! Why are they doing that?" cried Alice in distress.

"They are from the same place as the fruit. They are *dreamflowers*."

On the left of Alice sat the Duchess, who was next to her Cook. On the other side of the Cook was the Mock Turtle. He looked uncomfortable and nervous with such a neighbour, as the Cook kept glancing at him hungrily, as if she would like to turn him into a soup, and sprinkle him generously with pepper.

Opposite him sat the Gryphon, who appeared, even here, anxious to give Lessons to the Mock Turtle.

As Alice watched, the Gryphon was writing something on a small wooden-framed slate. He held it up to the Mock Turtle, and Alice could see that the letters were:—

H—A—R—M.

"Now, what does that spell?" he said to the Mock Turtle.

"It is Charm without the C," he replied.

"Very good," said the Gryphon approvingly.

He rubbed the letters out with a moistened finger and wrote something else.

He displayed the slate to the Mock Turtle. Alice saw that he had written:—

E—V—I—L.

"What does *that* spell?"

The Mock Turtle looked solemnly at the mysterious letters. "Why, it's 'LIVE', backwards!" he exclaimed.

Alice thought it was indeed, but the Gryphon was less impressed this time.

"How did you manage to see that?"

"I just twiddled my eyes, and then I saw it directly."

On Alice's right was the Hatter, with the March Hare next to *him*. Opposite her further down the table were Tweedledum and Tweedledee, and further *still* the Red King and Queen.

The Red Queen smiled and inclined her head graciously when she spotted Alice. But the head of the Red King was cradled in his arms as he leaned forward on the table, fast asleep.

Pointing at him, Tweedledum said in a loud whisper to Alice:—

"Dreaming all this *he* is. That's how *you're* here. We'd better not wake him—or there'll be no Banquet!"

"We *could* wake him for the *lecture*, though," suggested Tweedledee.

"Too much of a risk," said Tweedledum. "He might not go back to sleep quickly enough, and we'd miss the First Course!"

"Oh," thought Alice, "it's *that* sort of Lecture the White Knight meant when I asked him what present he was giving the Queen of Hearts.·Not 'a reproof or reprimand', but 'a formal expository or instructive discourse before an.audience'. Well! That makes a *lot* more sense, and should be far more agreeable to her Majesty!"

Alice was surprised to discover that she could hear snatches of conversation from near *and* distant parts of the table. Sometimes from her right. Sometimes from her left. Some voices she thought she recognized. Others she definitely did not.

"Whereabouts are we just now—and *who* are we, beginning with me?"

"This is Alice, Sir; and *this* is the Boy who slew the Jabberwock."

"Ah yes! I know *them* well enough!" the elderly voice murmured. "It's *myself* I'm most anxious about."

"Well, well! Then the Party shall be held without you!"

"Better so, than if it were held *within* me!" the other voice murmured with a bewildered air, as if he hardly knew what he was saying.

"He is *very* clever. Sometimes he says things no one but he can understand. Sometimes he says things not even *he* can understand!"

"How sorry *is* she?" a voice asked.
"Three quarters of a yard," came the solemn reply.

"I hope you have had a good night, my child."
"I've had the same night *you've* had," he replied. "There's only been *one* night since yesterday!"

"The boy's such an idiot," a voice declared firmly.
"*Idiot* indeed!" cried a female voice in protest. "He's no more an idiot than I am."
"You're right, my dear," came the soothing reply. "He isn't, indeed!"

"I lost my shoe on the way here, and I'm hopping to find another."
"Do you mean 'hopping', or 'hoping'?"
"Both!"

"What did you say the Ambassador's name was?"
"His Adiposity the Baron Doppelgeist."
"Why does he come with such a funny name?"
"He couldn't well change it on the journey, because of the luggage."

"Just see what a short way back it is," said a voice that sounded like the Red Queen's. "Why, if you started tomorrow morning, you'd be there in very little more than a week!"
"It took me a full month to *come*," a male voice replied incredulously.
"Yes. But it's ever so much shorter, going *back*, you know. You can go back *five* times, in the time it took you to come here *once*—if you start tomorrow morning!"

Alice said quietly to the White Knight: "There seems to be an unusual amount of *mad* people here."

"The number of lunatics," began the White Knight amiably, "is becoming greater every year."

"Isn't that a little *alarming?*" asked Alice.

"Not at all. When ninety per cent of us are lunatics, the asylums will be put to their proper use."

"And that is?" Alice gravely enquired.

"To shelter the sane!" said the White Knight. "We shall bar ourselves in. The lunatics will have it all their own way, *outside*. They'll do it a little queerly, no doubt. Railway collisions will be always happening: steamers always blowing up: most of the towns will be burnt down: most of the ships sunk—"

"And most of the people *killed*!" protested Alice unhappily.

"Certainly," the White Knight assented. "Till at last there will be *fewer* lunatics than sane men. Then *we* come out: *they* go in: and things return to their normal condition."

Why were the stories she heard, thought Alice, so often about disappointment or disaster? The songs and poems too, she realized.

The Pig's unsuccessful attempt to jump.

King Fisher's unsuccessful courtship of Lady Bird.

The Little Man and his Gun, and the Tale of Peter and Paul, which certainly, ended in disaster for the Duck and Peter! Even the Song of the Three Badgers, which ended happily, had been about the badgers and fish disappointing their parents. And what about her own poem about the little birds? It had included fish being shot and birds eaten by stags—

Alice saw that on the other side of the Duchess, her Cook was now perusing a large Cookery Book, making the Mock Turtle more nervous than ever, and reminding Alice of the little birds again—

Little Birds are writing
Interesting books
To be read by cooks:
Read, I say, not—

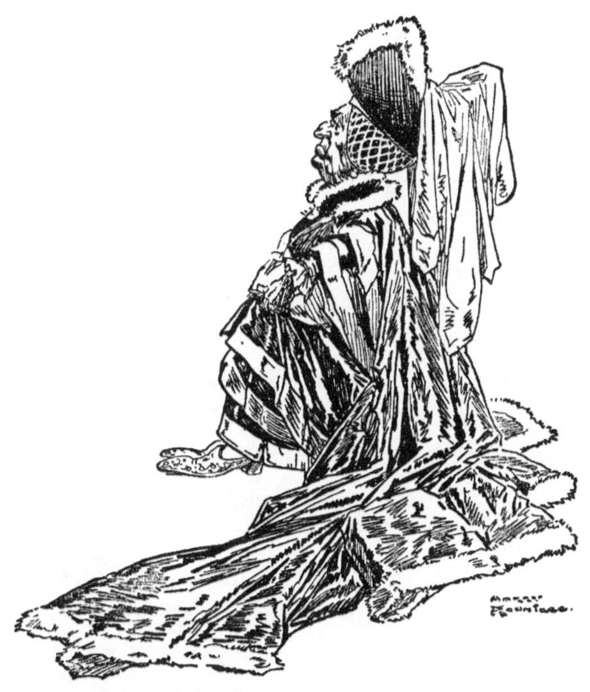

The Duchess (who wore the longest cloak Alice had ever seen) turned and said, "Did you roast it?"

"Roast what?"

"The pig."

Alice realized she meant the pig she had taken from the Duchess's kitchen long ago.

"Certainly not," said Alice, shocked.

"What a waste! Always remember"—

"Wilful waste makes woeful want,
and you may live to say
'How much I wish I had the crust
that then I threw away!'

"And you know what the moral to that is, don't you?'

"What is it?"

"'Always look where it goes to'!"

"Where *what* goes to?" was Alice's astonished reply.

"The crust you threw away!" said the Duchess. "Then if you lived to say 'How much I wish I had the crust—' you'd know where to find it."

Alice certainly remembered where the pig had 'gone to'—into the Wood—but she thought it unlikely she would ever find it again.

On the other side of the Boy sat the White Queen, and on the right of *her* sat the White King. The latter now stood up, and all the snatches of conversation ceased. There was an instant silence through the Banqueting Hall. They evidently expected a speech.

"Ahem. Ahem. Ahem. Welcome, my dear Fellows—"

"Don't call them names!" whispered the White Queen. "They wo'n't like it!"

"I said 'Fellows', not 'Felons'," he replied.

"My dear Fellows," he began again, referring to what Alice recognized to be his memorandum book, "you may be sure that I always sympa—" ("Hear! Hear!" shouted the crowd, so loud as to quite drown the orator's thin, squeaky voice) "—that I always sympa—" he repeated. ("Don't simper quite so much!" said the White Queen. "It makes you sound idiotic!" And, all this time, "Hear! Hear!" went rumbling round the room, like a peal of thunder.)

"That I always *sympathize!*" yelled the White King, the first moment there was silence. "But your true friends are the King and Queen of Hearts. Day and Night they are brooding on your wrongs—I should say your *rights*—that is to say your *wrongs*—no, I mean your *rights*—"

"Don't say any more," said the White Queen urgently. "You're making a mess of it!"

The White King took a deep breath, then said, "I am *honoured* to introduce—"

"*Honoured!*" the White Queen exclaimed. "That's better. You're a born orator, my dear. Bravo!"

"Thank you. But most orators are *born*, you know," he whispered back. "And please stop talking. It interrupts me so!" Raising his voice he continued: "I am *honoured* to introduce the White Knight to give us the Royal Birthday

Lecture. He has never lectured before—" (loud cheers) "—and will never lecture again" (even louder cheers).

He abruptly sat down and the White Knight stood up.

There was an awkward pause: he evidently didn't know how to begin. The White Queen looked up at him over the Boy's head.

"It's difficult to get things started," she whispered. "When once you get started, it'll go all right, you'll see. Try a joke. Just to put people at their ease, you know."

"True, true, Madam!" the White Knight meekly replied. He turned to the crowd and addressed them in a loud voice.

"Learn your A.'s!" he shouted. "Your B's! Your C's! And your D's! *Then* you'll be at your ease!"

There was a roar of laughter from the assembly, and then a great deal of confused whispering. "*What* was it he said? Something about bees, I fancy——-"

Then everyone became quiet as he began his long-awaited Lecture.

CHAPTER VIII

A Mad Lecture

"In Science—in fact, in most things—it is usually best *to begin at the beginning*. In *some* things, of course, it's better to begin at the *other* end. For instance, if you wanted to paint a dog green, it *might* be best to begin with the *tail*, as it doesn't bite at *that* end. And so—"

"May *I* help you?" the Boy interrupted.

"Help me to do *what?*" said the puzzled White Knight, looking up for a moment, but keeping his finger on the book he was reading from, so as not to lose his place.

"To paint a dog green!" cried the Boy. "*You* can begin with his mouth, and I'll—"

"No, no!" said the White Knight. "We haven't got to the *experiments* yet. And so," returning to his note-book, "I'll give you the Axioms of Science. After that I shall exhibit some Specimens. Then I shall explain a Process or two. And I shall conclude with a few Experiments. An *Axiom*, you know—from the Greek *axiōma*—is a thing you accept without contradiction. For instance, if I were to say 'Here we are!', that would be accepted without any contradiction, and it's a nice sort of remark to *begin* a conversation with. So it would be an *Axiom*. Or again, supposing I were to say 'Here we are not!', *that* would be—"

"—a fib!" cried the Boy.

"—be accepted, if people were civil," continued the White Knight; "so it would be *another* Axiom."

"It *might* be an Axeldum," the Boy said: "but it wouldn't be *true!*"

"Ignorance of Axioms," the Lecturer continued, "is a great drawback in life. It wastes so much time to have to say them over and over again. For instance—"

"I say, look here, you know!" interrupted the King of Hearts, who was getting a little restless. "How many Axioms are you going to give us? If you rattle on like this, we sha'n't get to the *experiments* till the middle of next week!"

"Oh, sooner than *that*, I assure you!" the White Knight replied, looking up in alarm. "There are only," (he referred to his notes again) "only *two* more, that are really *necessary*."

"Read 'em out, and get on to the *Specimens*," grumbled the King.

"The *first* Axiom," the White Knight read out in a great hurry, "consists of *these* words, '*Whatever is, is.*' And the

Second consists of *these* words, '*Whatever isn't, isn't.*' We will now go on to the *Specimens*. This tray contains Crystals and other Things." He drew it towards him, and again referred to his note-book. "Some of the labels—owing to insufficient adhesion—" Here he stopped again, and carefully examined the page with his eye-glass. "I ca'n't quite read the rest of the sentence," he said at last, "but it *means* the labels have come loose, and the Things have got mixed—"

"Let *me* stick 'em on again!" cried the Boy eagerly, and began licking them like postage-stamps, and dabbing them down upon the Crystals and the other Things. But the White Knight hastily moved the tray out of his reach. "They *might* get fixed to the *wrong* Specimens, you know!" he said.

"You shouldn't have any *wrong* Specimens on the tray!" the Boy boldly replied. "*Should* he?" he said, appealing to Alice.

But Alice only shook her head and said "Hush!"

The White Knight heard him not. He had taken up one of the bottles, and was carefully reading the label through his eye-glass. "Our first Specimen—" he announced, as he placed the bottle in front of the other Things, "is—that is, it is called—" here he took it up, and examined the label again, as if he thought it might have changed since he last saw it, "is called *aqua pura*—common water—the fluid that *cheers*—"

"*Hip! Hip! Hip!*" the Duchess's Cook began enthusiastically. "—but *not* inebriates!" the White Knight went on quickly, but only just in time to check the "*Hurrah!*" which was beginning. "Our second Specimen," he went on, carefully opening a small jar, "is—" here he removed the lid, and a large beetle instantly darted out, and with an angry buzz went straight out of the Pavilion, "—is—or rather, I should say," looking sadly into the empty jar, "it *was* a curious kind of Blue

Beetle. Did any one happen to remark—as it went past—three blue spots under each wing?"

Nobody had remarked them.

"Ah, well!" the White Knight said with a sigh. "It's a pity. Unless you remark that kind of thing *at the moment*, it's very apt to get overlooked! The *next* Specimen, at any rate, will not fly away! It is—in short, or perhaps, more correctly, at *length*—an Elephant. You will observe—" Here he beckoned to the three gardeners—Two, Five, and Seven—to come forward, and with their help began putting together what looked like an enormous dog-kennel, with short tubes projecting out of it on both sides.

"But we've seen *elephants* before," the King of Hearts grumbled.

"Yes, but not like *this*!" the White Knight eagerly replied. "You know you ca'n't see a *flea*, properly, without a *magnifying*-glass—what we call a *microscope*. Well, in just the same way, you ca'n't see an *elephant*, properly, without a *minimifying*-glass—what I call—all my own invention—a *megaloscope*! There's a minimifying-glass in each of these little tubes. The gardeners will now bring in the next Specimen. Please open *both* curtains, down at the end there, and make way for the Elephant!"

There was a general rush to the sides of the Pavilion, and all eyes were turned to the open end, watching the return of the three gardeners, who had gone away singing *"He thought he saw an elephant that practised on a fife!"* There was silence for a minute: and then their voices were heard again in the distance. *"He looked again*—come up, then! *He looked again and found it was*—whoa back! *And found it was a letter from his*—make way there! He's a-coming!" And in marched, or waddled—it was hard to say which is the right word—an Elephant, on its hind-legs, and playing on an enormous fife which it held with its forefeet.

The gardeners nimbly kept out of the Elephant's path, though Alice reflected, "It couldn't do them much harm. They're quite flat already. I wonder what they sleep in?" she continued to herself. "They wouldn't be comfortable in a real bed, you know, they are far too thin. They would be much happier in a portfolio, between sheets of blotting-paper, and each with a pen-wiper for a pillow."

The White Knight hastily threw open a large door at the end of the Megaloscope, and the huge animal, at a signal from one of the gardeners, dropped the fife, and obediently trotted into the machine, the door of which was at once shut by the White Knight. "The Specimen is now ready for observation!" he proclaimed. "It is exactly the size of the Common Mouse— *Mus Communis*!"

There was a general rush to the tubes, and the spectators watched with delight the minikin creature as it playfully coiled its trunk round the White Knight's extended finger, finally taking its stand upon the palm of his hand, in which position he carefully lifted it out for general exhibition.

"Isn't it a *darling?*" cried Alice. "May I pet it, please? I'll touch it *very* gently!"

The White Queen inspected it solemnly with her eye-glass. "It is very small," she said in a low voice. "Smaller than elephants usually are, I believe?"

The White Knight gave a start of delighted surprise. "Why, that's *true!*" he murmured to himself. Then louder, turning to the audience. "Her Imperial Highness has made a remark which is perfectly sensible!" And a wild cheer arose from that vast multitude.

"The next Specimen," the White Knight proclaimed, after carefully placing the little Elephant in the tray, among the Crystals and other Things, "is a *flea*, which we will enlarge for the purposes of observation."

Taking a small pill-box from the tray, he advanced to the Megaloscope, and reversed all the tubes.

"The Specimen is ready!" he cried, with his eye at one of the tubes, while he carefully emptied the pill-box through a little hole at the side. "The Flea is now the size of the Common Horse—*Equus Communis!*"

There was another general rush, to look through the tubes, and the Pavilion rang with shouts of delight, through which the White Knight's anxious tones could scarcely be heard. "Keep the door firmly *shut!*" he cried. "If the creature were to escape, *this size*, it would—" But the mischief was done. The door had swung open, and in another moment the Flea had got out, and was trampling down the terrified, shrieking spectators.

Three Experiments

But the White Knight's presence of mind did not desert him. "Undraw those curtains!" he shouted. It was done. The monster gathered its legs together, and in one tremendous bound vanished into the sky.

"Where *is* it?" said the King of Hearts, rubbing his eyes.

"In the next Province, I fancy," the White Knight replied. "That jump would take it at *least* five miles. It'll be quite comfortable in the Land of Giant Flowers. It's sure to find a house that suits it. The next thing is to explain a process or two. But I find there is hardly room enough to operate—the smaller animal is rather in my way—"

"Who does he mean?" the Boy whispered across the table to Alice.

"He means *you*!" Alice whispered back.

"Be kind enough to move—angularly—to *this* corner," the White Knight said, addressing himself to the Boy.

The Slayer of the Jabberwock hastily moved his chair in the direction indicated. "Did I move angrily enough?" he enquired. But the White Knight was once more absorbed in his Lecture, which he was reading from his note-book.

"I will now explain the Process of—the name is blotted, I'm sorry to say. It will be illustrated by a number of—of—" here he examined the page for some time, and at last said "It seems to be either 'Experiments' or 'Specimens'—"

"Let it be *Experiments*," said the King of Hearts. "We've seen plenty of *Specimens*."

"Certainly, certainly!" the White Knight assented. "We will have some Experiments."

"May *I* do them?" the Boy eagerly asked.

"Oh dear no!" The White Knight looked dismayed. "I really don't know what would happen if *you* did them!"

"Nor does anybody know what'll happen if *you* do them!" the Boy retorted.

THE FIRST EXPERIMENT

"Our First Experiment requires a Machine." He lifted a box out of the tray. "It has two knobs—only *two*—you can count them if you like."

The Duchess's Cook stepped forwards, counted them, and retired satisfied.

"Now you *might* press those two knobs together—but that's not the way to do it. Or you *might* turn the Machine upside-down—but *that's* not the way to do it!"

"What *is* the way to do it?" said the Boy, who was listening very attentively.

The White Knight smiled benignantly. "Ah, yes!" he said, in a voice like the heading of a chapter. "The Way To Do It! Permit me!" and in a moment he had whisked the Boy upon the tray. "I will divide my subject," he began, "into three parts—"

"I think I'll get down!" the Boy whispered to Alice. "It isn't nice to be divided! That's what I did to the Jabberwock!"

"He wo'n't hurt you, silly boy!" Alice responded confidently (though not perhaps advisedly), while the White Knight ordered:

"Stand still! You nearly squashed the Elephant! Though when I look more closely," he added, half to himself, "I see it isn't the Elephant at all, just a crumpled up sheet of writing-paper!" Then he resumed his instructions.

"The first part is to take hold of the knobs," he said, putting the objects into the Boy's hands. "The second part is—" Here he turned a handle on the box, and, with a loud "Oh!" the Boy dropped both the knobs, and began rubbing his elbows.

The White Knight chuckled in delight. "It had a sensible effect. *Hadn't* it?" he enquired.

"No, it hadn't a *sensible* effect!" the Boy said indignantly. "It was very silly indeed. It jingled my elbows, and it banged my back, and it crinkled my hair, and it buzzed among my bones!"

"I'm sure it *didn't*!" said Alice. "You're only inventing!"

"You don't know anything about it!" the Boy replied. "You weren't there to see. Nobody can go among my bones. There isn't room!"

THE SECOND EXPERIMENT

"Our Second Experiment," the White Knight announced, as the Boy returned to his place, still thoughtfully rubbing his elbows, "is the production of that seldom-seen-but-greatly-to-be-admired phenomenon, Black Light! You have seen White Light, Red Light, Green Light, and so on: but never, till this wonderful day, have any eyes but mine seen *Black Light*! This box," carefully lifting it upon the table, and covering it with a heap of blankets, "is quite full of it. The way I made it was this—I took a lighted candle into a dark cupboard and shut the door. Of course the cupboard was then full of *Yellow* Light. Then I took a bottle of Black ink, and poured it over the candle—and, to my delight, every atom of the Yellow Light turned *Black*! That was indeed the proudest moment of my life! Then I filled a box with it. And now—would anyone like to get under the blankets and see it?"

Dead silence followed this appeal: but at last the Boy said "*I'll* get under, if it wo'n't jingle my elbows."

Satisfied on this point, the Boy crawled under the blankets, and, after a minute or two, crawled out again, very hot and dusty, and with his hair in the wildest confusion.

"What did you see in the box?" Alice eagerly asked.

"I saw *nothing*!" the Boy sadly replied. "It was too dark!"

"He has described the appearance of the thing exactly!" the White Knight exclaimed with enthusiasm. "Black Light, and Nothing, look so extremely alike, at first sight, that I don't wonder he failed to distinguish them! We will now proceed to the Third Experiment."

The Third Experiment

"One can easily imagine a situation," began the White Knight, "where, under the right conditions, *anything*, no matter how *heavy*, would be *light*—"

"How could it be?" cried Alice eagerly. "Tell us the answer to such a paradox. We shall never guess it!"

"Well, suppose this Pavilion, just as it is, placed a few billion miles above a planet, with nothing else near enough to disturb it: of course it falls to the planet?"

Alice nodded. "Of course—though it might take some centuries to do it."

"Well now, supposing tea-time were going on all the while it was falling, falling, falling. If I were to take a cup of tea, and hold it out at arm's length, of course I feel its *weight*. It is trying to fall, and I prevent it. And, if I let go, it falls to the floor. But, if we were all falling together, it couldn't be trying to fall any quicker, you know: for, if I let go, what more could it do, than fall? And as my hand would be falling too—at the same rate—it would never leave it, for that would be to get ahead of it in the race. And it could never overtake the falling floor!"

"I see it clearly," said Alice. "But it makes one dizzy to think of such things!"

"Let us further imagine," the White Knight continued, "a cord fastened to the Pavilion, from below, and pulled down by someone on the planet. Then of course the *Pavilion* goes faster than its natural rate of falling; but the furniture—the table carrying the tea-things, and the chairs carrying our good selves—would go on falling at their old pace, and would therefore be left behind."

"Meaning we should all rise till we hit our heads on the ceiling!" exclaimed Alice.

"To avoid that," said the White Knight, "we could have the table and chairs fixed to the floor, and ourselves tied down to the chairs. Then we could all drink our cups of tea in peace. With only one drawback! We could take the *cups* down with us: but what about the tea? *That* would rise to the ceiling—unless we chose to drink it on the way! Now, observe—"

The White Knight left the table, and led the way to where Alice remembered the Elephant's large fife had fallen. On this spot now stood a post that had been driven firmly into the floor. To one side of the post was fastened a chain, with an iron weight hooked on to the end of it, and from the other side projected a piece of whalebone, with a ring at the end of it. "This is a *most* interesting Experiment!" the White Knight announced. "It will need *time*, I'm afraid: but that is a trifling disadvantage. Now observe. If I were to un-hook this weight, and let go, it would fall to the ground. You do not deny *that*?"

Nobody denied it.

"And in the same way, if I were to bend this piece of whalebone round the post—thus—and put the ring over this hook—thus—it stays bent: but, if I unhook it, it straightens itself again. You do not deny *that*?"

Again, nobody denied it.

"Well, now, suppose we left things just as they are, for a long time. The force of the *whalebone* would get exhausted, you know, and it would stay bent, even when you unhooked it. Now, *why* shouldn't the same thing happen with the *weight*? If a *whalebone* can be bent so long it has stopped trying to straighten itself, why ca'n't a *weight* be held up so long it has stopped trying to fall? That's what *I* want to know!"

"That's what *we* want to know!" echoed the crowd.

"How long must we wait?" grumbled the King of Hearts.

The White Knight looked at his watch. "Well, I *think* a thousand years will do to *begin* with," he said. "Then we will cautiously unhook the weight: and, if it *still* shows (as perhaps it will) a *slight* tendency to fall, we will hook it on to the chain again, and leave it for *another* thousand years."

Here the White Queen experienced one of those flashes of Common Sense which were the surprise of all around her.

"Meanwhile," she said, rising to her feet, "we can begin the Banquet."

"We can *indeed*!" cried the delighted White Knight. "Let the Banquet be served!"

The White Queen looked much pleased, and tried to clap her hands: but she might as well have knocked two feather-beds together, for any noise it made.

The Banquet

No time was lost in helping the dishes, and very speedily every guest found his plate filled with good things.

"I have always maintained the principle," the White Knight began, "that it is a good rule to take some food—occasionally. The great advantage of dinner-parties—" he broke off suddenly. "Why, actually here's Humpty Dumpty!" he cried. "And there's no place left for him!"

Humpty Dumpty crossed the room reading his large Dictionary, which he held close to his eyes. One result of his not looking where he was going was that he caught his foot in the Duchess's long cloak, flew up into the air, and fell heavily on his face in the middle of the table.

"*What* a pity!" cried the kind-hearted White Knight as he helped him up. "Of course, if you go about like that, you must expect to tumble. You should look. You never do! You always walk with your chin in the air."

"It wouldn't be *me*, if I didn't trip," said Humpty Dumpty.

The White Knight looked much shocked. "Almost *anything* would be better than *that*!" he exclaimed. "It never does," he added, aside to the Boy, "to be anybody else, does it?"

A place was found for Humpty Dumpty between the Boy and the White Queen (Alice remembered that the White King and Queen had once given Humpty Dumpty a cravat as an un-birthday present, so must know him quite well), but his chair had to be *very* big.

The Boy found him a rather uninteresting neighbour: in fact, when Alice asked him later if he'd had any conversation with him, he replied "All he's said so far is 'What a comfort a Dictionary is!' and I replied 'Yes, Sir.' I don't believe *that* deserves to be called a 'conversation' at all."

"Another advantage of dinner-parties," the White Knight cheerfully explained, for the benefit of anyone that would listen, "is that it helps you to see your friends. If you want to *see* a man, offer him something to eat. It's the same rule with a mouse."

"And with a cat," said the Hatter. And turning to Alice, he said, "Please pour some milk in your saucer. Kittie's ever so thirsty!"

"Why do you want *my* saucer," said Alice. "You've got one yourself!"

"Yes, I know," said the Hatter: "but I wanted *mine* for to give it some *more* milk in."

Alice was unconvinced; however, she quietly filled her saucer with milk, and put it in the middle of the table.

Immediately the head of the Cheshire-Cat appeared, and grinned widely at Alice.

It then commenced lapping up the milk, but as only the *front* part of its body followed, where the milk *went* Alice was puzzled to know. "Where does the milk *go?*" she asked the Hatter.

But the Hatter did not hear the question.

"There's somebody scratching at the door and wanting to come in," he said. And he scrambled down off his chair, and went and cautiously peeped out through the door-way.

"Who was it wanted to come in?" Alice asked as he returned to his place.

"It was The Dormouse," said the Hatter. "And it peeped in. And it saw the Cheshire-Cat. And it said 'I'll come back another time.' And I said 'You needn't be frightened. This cat is *very* kind to mice.' And it said 'But I've got some important business that I *must* attend to.' And it said 'I'll call again later.' And it said 'Give my love to the Cheshire-Cat.'"

Alice remembered the mouse she'd met in the Pool of Tears, and its reaction when Alice spoke to it about her cat catching mice: "Would *you* like cats if you were me? Our family always *hated* cats: nasty, low, vulgar things! Don't let me hear the name again!"

"If this cat is kind to mice," said Alice, "it must be a very singular cat."

"It's less than singular at the moment. There's only half of it here. The more it drinks, the smaller it gets. But I know it *is* kind to mice. Because it plays with them; for to amuse them, you know."

"But that is just what I *don't* know," Alice rejoined. "My belief *is,* cats play with mice to *kill* them!"

"Oh, that's quite an *accident*!" the Hatter began, so eagerly, that it was evident he had already propounded this very difficulty to the Cat. "It explained all that to me. It said 'I teach the mice new games: the mice like it ever so much.' It said 'Sometimes little accidents happen: sometimes the mice kill themselves.' It said 'I'm always *very* sorry, when the mice kill themselves.' It said—"

"If it was so *very* sorry," Alice said, rather disdainfully, "*it* wouldn't *eat* the mice after they'd killed themselves!"

But this difficulty, also, had evidently not been lost sight of by the Hatter. "It answered that very question just now, in between drinking the milk. It said—" (the Hatter constantly omitted, as superfluous, his own share of the dialogue, and merely gave the replies of the Cat) "It said 'Dead mice *never* object to being eaten.' It said 'There's no use wasting good mice.' It said:—

> *"Wilful waste makes woeful want,*
> *and you may live to say*
> *"How much I wish I had the mouse*
> *that then I threw away!"'*

It said—"

"It hadn't *time* to say such a lot of things!" Alice interrupted indignantly.

"Cats speak *very quickly*!" he rejoined contemptuously. "Look how fast its tongue moves!"

All that was left of the Cheshire-Cat was its mouth. And Alice had to admit its tongue *did* move very quickly as it lapped up the milk.

"*You* don't *hear* quickly enough," said the Hatter.

Then the milk—and the mouth—both fully disappeared together.

The Banquet continued in comparative silence, till the White King raised the cover from an enormous dish.

"What is it?" the White Queen said faintly, as she put her spy-glass to her eye. "Why, it's *spinach*, I declare!"

She took up her spoon in an absent manner, and tried to balance it across the back of her hand, and in doing this she dropped it into the dish: and, when she took it out again, it was full of spinach.

"How curious!" she said, and put it into her mouth. "It tastes just like *real* spinach! I thought it was an imitation—but I do believe it's real!" And she took another spoonful.

"It wo'n't be real much longer," said the Boy.

The White Knight cut a large slice of cake, put it on the Boy's plate, and gazed at his own empty plate in astonishment.

"Where did you get that cake?" Alice whispered.

"*He* gave it me."

"But you shouldn't ask for things! You *know* you shouldn't!"

"I *didn't* ask," said the Boy, taking a fresh mouthful: "He *gave* it me."

Alice considered this for a moment: then she saw her way out of it.

"Well, then, ask him to give *me* some!"

"You seem to enjoy that cake," the White Knight remarked.

"Does that mean 'like'?" the Boy whispered to Alice.

Alice nodded. "Enjoy means 'to eat' and 'to *like* to eat'."

The Boy smiled at the White Knight. "I *do* enjoy it," he said.

The White Queen caught the word. "And I hope you're enjoying *yourself*, little man?" she enquired.

The Boy's look of horror quite startled her. "No, *indeed* I am not!" he said.

The White Queen looked thoroughly puzzled. "Well, well," she said. "Try some cowslip wine!" And she filled a glass and handed it to the Boy. "Drink this, my dear, and you'll be quite another man!"

"Who shall I be?" said the Boy, pausing in the act of putting it to his lips.

"Don't ask so many questions!" Alice interposed, anxious to save the poor White Queen from further bewilderment. "Suppose we get someone to tell us a story?"

The Boy adopted the idea with enthusiasm. "*Please* do!" he cried eagerly. "Something about tigers—and bumble-bees—and robin red-breasts, you know!"

"Why should you always have *live* things in stories?" said Humpty Dumpty, putting down his Dictionary at last. "Why don't you have events, or circumstances?"

"Oh, *please* invent a story like that!" cried the Boy.

Humpty Dumpty began fluently enough. "Once a coincidence was taking a walk with a little accident, and they met an explanation—a *very* old explanation—so old that it was quite doubled up, and looked more like a conundrum—" he broke off suddenly.

"*Please* go on!" both children exclaimed.

Humpty Dumpty made a candid confession. "It's a very difficult sort to invent, I find. Suppose the Dormouse tells us a story instead." Alice was very surprised to see that the Dormouse was seated between the Hatter and the March Hare. He must have returned without her noticing, and when he saw that the Cheshire-Cat had safely departed, joined them at the table.

Without any hesitation, he began: "Once there was a Mouse—a little tiny Mouse—such a tiny little Mouse! You never saw such a tiny Mouse—"

"Did nothing ever happen to it?" Alice asked. "Haven't you anything more to tell us, besides its being so tiny?"

"Nothing ever happened to it," the Dormouse solemnly replied.

"Why did nothing ever happen to it?" said Alice.

"It was too tiny," the Dormouse explained.

"*That's* no reason!" Alice said. "However tiny it *was*, things might happen to it."

The Dormouse looked pityingly at her, as if he thought her stupid.

"It was too tiny," he repeated. "If anything happened to it, it would die— it was so *very* tiny!"

"Really that's enough about its being tiny!" Alice put in. "Haven't you invented any more about it?"

"I haven't invented any more yet."

"Well then, you shouldn't begin a story till you've invented more!"

"*I'll* tell you a story!" the Boy began in a great hurry. "Once there was a Locust, and a Magpie, and an Engine-driver. And the Lesson is, to learn to get up early—"

"It isn't a bit interesting!" said Alice. "You shouldn't put the lesson so soon."

"'What must be must be'," said the Duchess, "and the moral of *that* is, 'What mustn't be mustn't be'."

"When did you invent that story?" Alice asked the Boy. "A minute ago?"

"*No!*" said the Boy. "A deal shorter ago than that. Guess again!"

"I ca'n't guess," said Alice, thinking it couldn't be shorter ago than *that*. "How long ago?"

"Why, it isn't invented yet!" the Boy exclaimed triumphantly. "But I *have* invented a lovely one! Shall I say it?"

"If you've *finished* inventing it," said Alice. "And let the Lesson be 'to try again'!"

"No," said the Boy with great decision. "The Lesson is '*Not* to try again'! Once there was a lovely china man, who stood on the chimney-piece. And he stood, and he stood. And one day he tumbled off, and he didn't hurt himself one bit. Only he *would* try again. And the next time he tumbled off, he hurt himself very much—"

"But how did he come back on the chimney-piece after his first tumble?" said Humpty Dumpty, rather sharply.

"*I* put him there!" cried the Boy.

"Then I'm afraid you know something about his tumbling," said Humpty Dumpty. "Perhaps you pushed him?"

To which the Boy replied, very seriously, "I didn't push him *much*—he was a *lovely* china man," he continued hastily, evidently very much anxious to change the subject. "Only in fun, you know," he added, blushing. "How warm it's getting in here!"

"The room's very hot, with all this crowd," said the White Knight. "I have an invention that would solve the problem beautifully. I wonder why they don't put some lumps of ice in the grate? You fill it with lumps of coal in the winter, you know, and you sit around it and enjoy the warmth. How jolly it would be to fill it now with lumps of ice, and sit round it and enjoy the coolth!"

"It's cold outside, though," said Alice. "When I was walking through the wood, my feet got quite cold."

"And that's the *Shoemaker's* fault!" the White Knight cheerfully replied. "How often I've explained to him that he *ought* to make boots with little iron frames under the soles, to hold lamps! But he never *thinks*. No one would suffer from cold, if only they would *think* of those little things. I always write with hot ink, in the winter. Very few people ever think of *that*. Yet how simple it is! And that reminds me! I left off writing at a comma. I'll be glad to get back and see how the sentence finishes. It's so awkward not knowing—"

By this time the appetites of the guests seemed to be nearly satisfied, and even the Boy had the resolution to say, when the White Knight offered him a fourth slice of plum-pudding, "I think three helpings is enough."

The White King stood up again. "Ahem!" he said.

"The entertainment will conclude," he announced, "with her Majesty's Birthday Treat. *Bits of Shakespeare*. All to be done by the Boy who slew the Jabberwock, with the assistance of the White Knight—and—ahem!—Alice!"

"Oh dear!" thought Alice, rising up in alarm. "Why do they want *me*?"

Fortunately Alice had participated in many family theatricals featuring Shakespeare, so as the shock of the announcement wore off, she began to feel a little less nervous.

"Will he *say* all the Bits of Shakespeare?" she asked the White Knight as she followed him to one of the sides of the room, where the Boy went through a door in it to dress for the first 'Bit'.

"No, he'll only *act* them," he replied. "He hardly knows any of the words. This is his birthday gift to the Queen."

"And what part must I play?"

"When we see what he's dressed like, we've to tell everyone what character it is. I'll do the first two to show you how it's done. Everyone's in such a hurry to guess! Don't you hear them all saying 'What? What? "' And so indeed they were: though till the White Knight explained it, it had sounded to Alice more like frogs croaking 'Wawt? Wawt?' in different parts of the Hall.

"But why do they try to guess it before they see it?"

"I don't know," the White Knight said: "but they always *do*. Sometimes the audiences begin guessing weeks and weeks before the day."

However, the chorus of guessing was cut short by the Boy, who suddenly rushed out from behind the door, and with a flying leap landed among them.

"Hamlet!" the White Knight proclaimed, and the 'croaking' all ceased in a moment. Alice watched in some curiosity to see what the Boy's ideas were as to the behaviour of Shakespeare's great Character. According to this eminent interpreter of the Drama, Hamlet sore a short black cloak (which he chiefly used for muffling up his face, as if he suffered a good deal from toothache), and turned out his toes very much as he walked. "To be or not to be!" Hamlet remarked in a cheerful tone, and then turned head-over-heels several times, his cloak dropping off in the performance.

Alice felt a little disappointed: the Boy's conception of the part seemed so wanting in dignity. "Wo'n't he say any more of the speech?" she whispered to the White Knight.

"I *think* not," he whispered in reply. "He generally turns head over heels when he doesn't know any more words."

The Boy had meanwhile settled the question by disappearing to change his costume; and the audience instantly began inquiring the name of the next Character.

"You'll know directly!" cried the White Knight (amid the chorus of "Wawt? Wawt?"). "Macbeth!" he proclaimed, as the Boy re-appeared. Macbeth had something twisted round him, that went over one shoulder and under the other arm, and was meant, Alice believed, for a Scotch plaid. Equally twisted was a dagger he held in his hand, which made Alice think he had borrowed the one belonging to the Queen of Clubs. He held it out at arm's length, as if he were a little afraid of it. "Is this a *dagger*?" Macbeth inquired, in a puzzled sort of tone, as if noticing its buckled and bent appearance.

Shakespeare had never revealed, as far as Alice knew, that Macbeth had any such eccentric habit of turning head-over-heels in private life: but the Boy evidently considered it quite an essential part of the character, and ended the portrayal with a series of somersaults, the last of which took him back through the door. However, he was through it again in a few moments, having tucked under his chin a tuft of wool, that nearly reached down to his feet. It made a magnificent beard, and seemed as light as the wool cultivated by Humpty Dumpty.

In all the excitement Alice nearly forgot that the time had come for her own contribution.

"Shylock!" Alice announced. "No, I beg your pardon!" she hastily corrected herself, "King Lear! I hadn't noticed the crown." (The Boy had very cleverly provided one, made out of gold paper.)

King Lear folded his arms (to the imminent peril of his beard) and said, in a mild explanatory tone, "Ay, every *inch* a king!" and then paused, as if to consider how this could be proved. And here, with all possible deference to the Boy as a Shakespearean critic, Alice had to express (privately) her opinion that the Bard had *never* intended his three great tragic heroes to be so strangely alike in their personal habits; nor did she believe that he would have accepted the faculty of turning head-over-heels as any proof at all of royal descent. Yet it appeared that King Lear, after deep meditation, could think of no other argument by which to prove his kingship: and, as this was the last of the 'Bits' of Shakespeare ("We never do more than *three*," the White Knight explained in a whisper), the Boy gave the audience quite a long series of somersaults before he finally retired, leaving the enraptured spectators all crying out "More! More!" which Alice supposed was their way of encoring a performance. But the Boy refused their entreaties, and after removing his costume, re-appeared in his real character to take his seat opposite Alice.

"A *lovely* gift for the Queen," she said to him approvingly, feeling in her pocket that the silver pin-cushion was quite safe. Then turning to the Hatter she said: "What present did *you* bring the Queen for her birthday?"

"Butter," he replied.

"The *best* butter," the March Hare added.

"To show we love no one *but her*," the Hatter explained.

"Life, what is it *but a* dream?" said the Dormouse sleepily.

"It usually is, for you," replied the Hatter. "You're nid-nid-nodding already. But—"

He looked around the room.

"—where *is* her Majesty?"

CHAPTER XI

Her Imperial Fatness

Suddenly the White Knight started as if he had been electrified. "Why, I had nearly forgotten the most important part of the proceedings. The Queen of Hearts! Why, it's *her* birthday, don't you know. And her health must be drunk, and all that sort of thing. What is the Queen's Birthday Party without the Queen?"

"Nicer," said the Boy.

Everybody had forgotten the Queen of Hearts!

"Is she *lost?*" said the Duchess anxiously. "Where can she

be?" The White King said, "She" (indicating the White Queen) "once lost *herself* in the Woods."

"And couldn't she find herself again?" said the Boy. "Why didn't she shout? She'd be sure to hear herself, 'cause she couldn't be far off, you know."

Humpty Dumpty picked up his Dictionary, and holding it upside down shook the pages.

"The Queen of Hearts isn't in *there*!" said Alice scornfully.

"Of course she isn't," he replied. "If she *was* she'd have fallen out by now. Do we *need* to find her? I once tried to find a Hippopotamus at the White Queen's house, but now I'm glad I didn't. If he'd dined with us today, there wouldn't have been much for us."

Their concern, once raised, quickly communicated itself to the entire room, and finally reached the King of Hearts.

"She *was* told of the Banquet, of course?" said the King of Hearts.

"Undoubtedly!" replied the White Knight. "*That* would be the duty of the Queen's Herald, the White Rabbit."

"Let the White Rabbit come forward!" the King gravely said. The White Rabbit came forwards, carrying a fan and gloves, which he immediately put into Alice's hands.

As soon as he'd done this, the appearance of the Rabbit began to change. In place of the fan and gloves came a trumpet and scroll, and in place of his normal clothes appeared a Herald's uniform.

"I attended on her Imperial Fatness," was the statement made by the trembling official. "I told her of the Lecture and the Banquet—"

"What followed?" said the King: for the unhappy creature seemed almost too frightened to go on.

The White Rabbit unrolled the parchment and read aloud the words:—

"'*Item*, her Imperial Fatness was graciously pleased to be sulky.'

"'*Item*, her Imperial Fatness was graciously pleased to lift me by my ears.'

"'*Item*, her Imperial Fatness was graciously pleased to say: I don't care!'"

"'Don't-care' came to a bad end," Alice whispered to the Boy. "I'm not sure, but I *believe* he was hanged."

The White Knight overheard her. "*That* result," he blandly remarked, "was merely a case of mistaken identity."

Both children looked puzzled.

"Permit me to explain. 'Don't-care' and 'Care' were twin brothers. 'Care', you know, killed the Cat. And they caught 'Don't-care' by mistake, and hanged him instead. And so 'Care' is alive still. But he's very unhappy without his brother. That's why they say 'Begone, dull Care!'"

"Thank you!" Alice said heartily. "It's extremely interesting. Why, it seems to explain everything!"

"Well, not quite *everything*," the White Knight modestly rejoined. "To explain *everything*—especially one or two chemical formulas—would take rather longer—"

"What was your general impression as to her Imperial Fatness?" the King asked the White Rabbit.

"My impression was that her Imperial Fatness was getting more—"

"More *what*?"

All listened breathlessly for the next word. "More *prickly*!"

"She must be sent for *at once*!" the King exclaimed. "Tell her she's *late*."

And the White Rabbit was off, muttering "She's late! She's late!"

"No use! No use!" Alice heard a voice murmur.

It seemed to come from above her.

She looked up and saw the Cheshire-Cat smilingly shaking his head. He was becoming visible on top of the post the White Knight had lectured about. Or was he? When she looked again (having waited for his ears to appear, for she couldn't speak to him till *then*), the post had turned into the trunk of a tree, and the weight and whalebone were now its two branches, on which the Cheshire-Cat was seated.

"*Why* is it no use?" asked Alice.

But all he replied was "Heartless! Heartless!" as he faded away again.

Pale, trembling, speechless, the White Rabbit returned. "Well?" said the King. "Why does not the Queen appear?"

"One can easily guess," said the White Knight. "Her Imperial Fatness is, without a doubt, a little preoccupied."

The Boy turned a look of solemn enquiry on Alice. "What does that word mean?" he asked.

But no one took any notice of the question. They were all eagerly listening to the White Rabbit's reply.

"Please your Highness! Her Imperial Fatness is—" Not a word more could he utter.

The Duchess rose in an agony of alarm. "Let us go to her!" she cried. And there was a general rush for the door.

The Boy slipped off his chair in a moment. "May I go too?" he eagerly

asked. But the King did not hear the question, as the White Knight was speaking to him. "*Preoccupied*, your Majesty!" he was saying. "That is what she is, no doubt!"

"May I go and see her?" the Boy repeated. The King nodded assent, and the Boy ran off. In a minute or two he returned, slowly and gravely.

"Well?" said the King. "What's the matter with the Queen?" "She's—what *you* said," the Boy replied, looking at the White Knight. "That hard word. *Prickle-occupied.*"

"No! Not that word at all!" came from the returning crowd behind him. Then adding, in horrified tones: "*Porcupine!* That's the word! Her Majesty has turned into a Porcupiness! A bright red one!"

"A New Specimen!" exclaimed the delighted White Knight. "An example of *porto porcysis*. Pray let me go in. It should be labeled at once!"

But the three gardeners—Two, Five, and Seven—only pushed him back. "Label it indeed! Do you want to have your head bitten off?" they cried.

"Never mind about Specimens," said the King, pushing his way through the crowd. "Tell us how to keep her safe!"

"A large cage!" the White Knight replied promptly. "Bring a large cage," he said to the people generally, "on four wheels, with strong bars of steel, and a portcullis made to go up and down like a mouse-trap! Does anyone happen to have such a thing about him?" It didn't sound a likely sort of thing for anyone to have about him: however, they brought him one directly: curiously enough, there happened to be one standing in the gallery.

"Put it facing the opening of the door, and draw up the portcullis!"

This was done in a moment.

"Blankets now!" cried the White Knight. "This is a most interesting Experiment!"

There happened to be a pile of blankets close by: and the White Knight had hardly said the word, when they were all unfolded and held up like curtains all around. They were rapidly arranged in two rows, so as to make a dark passage, leading straight from the door to the mouth of the cage.

"Now fling the door open!" This did not need to be done: the fearful monster flung the door open for itself, and, with a yell like the whistle of a steam-engine, rushed into the cage.

"Down with the portcullis!" No sooner said the done: and all breathed freely once more, on seeing the porcupine safely caged.

The White Knight rubbed his hands in childish delight. "The Experiment has succeeded!" he proclaimed. "All that is needed now is for the gardeners to feed it three times a day and—"

"Never mind about its food just now!" the King interrupted. "Let us return to the Banquet."

The three gardeners wheeled the cage out of the room.

"She *is* prickly, certainly," the King continued, addressing Alice, "but she wo'n't hurt anyone. It'll wear off. It always does. She'll be better soon."

"Has it happened before?" asked Alice.

"Oh yes. See the fate of a prickly life! Sometimes the prickles become real ones. But we must remember that, however porcupiny, she is royal still! After this feast is over, I'm going to take a little present to her Majesty—just to soothe her, you know: it isn't pleasant living in a cage."

"What'll you give her for a birthday-present?" Alice enquired.

"A small saucer of chopped carrots," replied the King. "In giving birthday presents, *my* motto is—cheapness! I should think I save forty pounds a year by giving—oh, *what* is that noise?"

CHAPTER XII

Good-night, Wonderland

Terrible crashing sounds filled the air. The three gardeners rushed in.

"The Porcupine has broken loose! She burst the cage! She's getting bigger!"

A loud and horrible voice could be heard. It was a sort of mixture—there was the roaring of a lion, and the bellowing of a bull, and now and then a scream like a gigantic parrot. Struggling to express itself, it was incoherent at first. But the words soon became recognizable: *"Off with their heads! Off with their heads!"*

All along the gallery that led to the Queen's apartments, an excited crowd was surging to and fro, and the Babel of voices was deafening: against the door of the room a group of men were leaning, vainly trying to shut it—for some great animal inside was constantly bursting it half open, and there was a glimpse, before the men could push it back again, of the head of a furious wild beast, with great fiery eyes and gnashing teeth.

The Boy who Slew the Jabberwock rushed forward, and with a few judicious, poker-like jabs of his sword helped to keep the creature at bay. "The place is in an uproar!" he cried. "Tell the White Knight to come—and tell him to bring an uproarglass with him!" There was a lull as they heard the Porcupine move away from the door. Then a thunderous noise and a tremor in the ground indicated it had rolled itself into a ball, and in that form was approaching the door again.

"It is time," said the White Knight, "for my final Experiment. One that hopefully will *not* need a thousand years to take effect.

"For this, we must set up the Megaloscope where the cage was previously positioned."

This was quickly done. He opened it and adjusted the tubes. "To complete the Experiment, I will take a certain Alkali, or Acid—I forget which. Now you'll see what will happen when I Mix it with Some—" here he took up a bottle, and looked at it doubtfully "—when I mix it with—with Something—"

Here the King of Hearts interrupted impatiently. "What's the *name* of the stuff?"

"I don't remember the *name*," said the White Knight: "and the label has come off."

He emptied it quickly into the other bottle.

With a tremendous bang, both bottles flew to pieces, and the Pavilion was shaken to its foundations, bursting open the windows, extinguishing some of the lamps, and filling the air with clouds of smoke, which took strange shapes in the air, and seemed to form *birds*. Birds Alice knew. The Birds from the fireplace tiles. Almost simultaneously the door burst open, and the Porcupiness—rolled up in a gigantic red ball—hurtled into the Megaloscope: exploded out of the other end: and crashed into the dining-table, sending everyone flying up into the air. "Like ninepins," thought Alice. "Or should that be *ninety-times-nine-pins?*"

But Alice had no time to consider the question, for things were happening now at a bewildering rate.

The flock of birds swooped down and met the flying figures. Skilfully catching them—some in their beaks, some in their claws—they carried them out of the open windows.

Amid the brightly coloured birds, a dark one appeared, and descending on Tweedledum and Tweedledee, gripped them by a claw in each collar and carried them away. As they went, Alice heard them cry, "Wake up the Red King! Wake up the Red King!"

As others departed through the windows, Alice heard words she recognized hearing before—

> *"He thought he saw an Elephant,*
> *   That practised on a fife—"*

> *"He has loaded with bullet and powder:*
> *   His footfall is noiseless as air:*
> *But the voices grow louder and louder,*
> *   And bellow, and bluster, and blare.*
> *They bristle before him and after,*
> *   They flutter above and below,*
> *Shrill shriekings of lubberly laughter,*
> *   Weird wailings of woe!"*

> *"He looked again, and found it was*
> *   A Bear without a head—"*

> *"'Yet pins have heads,' said Lady Bird—*
> *Sing prunes, singe prawns, sing primrose-hill!*
> *   'And where you stick them in,*
> *   They stay, and thus a pin*
> *Is very much to be preferred—*
> *   To one that's never still!'"*

> *"Yet still he got the old reply,*
> *   'It is not quite convenient!'"*

> *"'Poor thing,' he said, 'poor silly thing!*
> *It's waiting to be fed.'"*

"And if, in other days and hours
Mid other fluffs and other flowers,
The choice were given me how to dine—
'Name what thou wilt: it shall be thine!'
*   Oh , then I see*
*   The life for me*
Ipwergis-Pudding to consume,
And drink the subtle Azzigoom!"

"He looked again, and found it was
*   A Hippopotomus—"*

"Uprose that Pig, and rushed, full whack,
*   Against the ruined pump:*
Rolled over like an empty sack,
And settled down upon his back,
While all his bones at once went 'Crack!'
*   It was a fatal jump."*

"'If this should stay to dine,' he said,
*   'There wo'n't be much for us!'"*

Alice somehow felt it was now her *own* turn to speak, and began reciting:—

"Little Birds are sleeping
*   All among the pins,*
Where the loser wins—"

before being interrupted by the sight of the Porcupine rolling towards her.

In fright, she gripped her apron-pocket with one hand, while with the other she raised the White Rabbit's fan (she had lost the gloves) protectively over her head.

But instead of the Porcupine getting bigger and bigger, it was getting smaller and smaller.

It shrank—and shrank—and shrank.

Till it was a tiny pig.

No! A tiny *silver* pig.

A cushion-backed silver pig. With the porcupine-quills all turned into the little pins sticking out of it.

*   *   *   *
*   *   *
*   *   *   *

A sudden gust swept away the whole scene, and Alice found herself sitting up on the rug staring at the fire in the grate.

The grip on her pocket had disturbed her silver pig pin-cushion, and it had jumped out: it lay on its side in front of the solitary hearth, where the poker had knocked over the tongs and the shovel and upset some of the coals, sending a cloud of smoke into the room.

As the smoke drifted away, she saw again the tiles around the fireplace, and the pictures of little birds. Red, Blue, Green, etc. And the two red animals. The Bear and the Porcupine.

She looked for the White Rabbit's fan, but to her regret it was nowhere to be found.

"So, either I've been dreaming about Wonderland," she said to herself, "and this is the reality. Or else I've really been in Wonderland, and this is a dream. Is Life itself a dream, I wonder!"

Alice sat quietly for a while, and saw all the characters she had visited pass like a procession through her mind.

And she knew they were passing out of her life. She would never see them again.

"No use to try and stop them!" she said to herself, as they passed away into the shadows. "Why, they ca'n't even *see* me any more!

"No use at all," she echoed with a sigh. "One would *like* to meet them again! But I feel, somehow, *that* can never be. They have passed out of *my* life forever!"

With particular sadness she saw the Boy who slew the Jabberwock disappear, turning head-over-heels as he went. She lifted her hand in a wave of farewell, and wiped away a tear.

"I wish you a very good-night, Wonderland. I betake myself to my bed—to dream—if that indeed I be not dreaming now."

No, Alice would never see the faces of Wonderland again.

But perhaps, in the fire, she *would* see a face.

The face of a White Knight.
Not young.
Not old.
Somewhere in between.
The face of *her* White Knight.
All Alice had to do was wait for him.

> *"And the banquet, so plainly provided,*
> *Shall round into rose-buds and rice."*

Is all our Life, then, but a dream
Seen faintly in the golden gleam
Athwart Time's dark resistless stream?

Bowed to the earth with bitter woe,
Or laughing at some toy peep-show,
We flutter idly to and fro.

Man's little Day in haste we spend,
And, from its merry noontide, send
No glance to meet the silent end.

The Westminster Alice, by H. H. Munro (Saki), 2010

Alice in Blunderland: An Iridescent Dream,
by John Kendrick Bangs, 2010

Simulations

Davy and the Goblin, by Charles Edward Carryl, 2010

The Admiral's Caravan, by Charles Edward Carryl, 2010

Gladys in Grammarland, by Audrey Mayhew Allen, 2010

Alice's Adventures in Pictureland, by Florence Adèle Evans, 2011

Folly in Fairyland, by Carolyn Wells, 2016

Rollo in Emblemland, by J. K. Bangs & C. R. Macauley, 2010

Phyllis in Piskie-land, by J. Henry Harris, 2012

Alice in Beeland, by Lillian Elizabeth Roy, 2012

Eileen's Adventures in Wordland, by Zillah K. Macdonald, 2010

Alice and the Time Machine, by Victor Fet, 2016

Алиса и Машина Времени (Alisa i Mashina Vremeni),
Alice and the Time Machine in Russian, tr. Victor Fet, 2016

Sewelliana

Sun-hee's Adventures Under the Land of Morning Calm,
by Victoria J. Sewell & Byron W. Sewell, 2016

선희의 조용한 아침의 나라 모험기
(Seonhuiui joyonghan achim-ui nala moheomgi),
Sun-hee in Korean, tr. Miyeong Kang, 2016

Alix's Adventures in Wonderland:
Lewis Carroll's Nightmare, by Byron W. Sewell, 2011

Áloþk's Adventures in Goatland, by Byron W. Sewell, 2011

Alice's Bad Hair Day in Wonderland, by Byron W. Sewell, 2012

The Carrollian Tales of Inspector Spectre, by Byron W. Sewell, 2011

Eachtraí Eilíse i dTír na nIontas, *Alice* in Irish, tr. Nicholas Williams, 2007

Lastall den Scáthán agus a bhFuair Eilís Ann Roimpi,
Looking-Glass in Irish, tr. Nicholas Williams, 2009

Le Avventure di Alice nel Paese delle Meraviglie,
Alice in Italian, tr. Teodorico Pietrocòla Rossetti, 2010

Alis Advencha ina Wandalan,
Alice in Jamaican Creole, tr. Tamirand Nnena De Lisser, 2016

L's Aventuthes d'Alice en Êmèrvil'lie,
Alice in Jèrriais, tr. Geraint Williams, 2012

L'Travèrs du Mitheux et chein qu'Alice y dêmuchit,
Looking-Glass in Jèrriais, tr. Geraint Williams, 2012

Әлисәнің ғажайып елдегі басынан кешкендері
(Älïsäniñ ğajayıp eldegi basınan keşkenderi),
Alice in Kazakh, tr. Fatima Moldashova, 2016

Алисанын Кызыктар Өлкөсүндөгү укмуштуу окуялары
(Alisanın Kızıktar Ölkösündögü ukmuştuu okuyaları),
Alice in Kyrgyz, tr. Aida Egemberdieva, 2016

Las Aventuras de Alisia en el Paiz de las Maraviyas,
Alice in Ladino, tr. Avner Perez, 2016

לאס אב׳ינטוראס די אליסייה אין איל פאיס די לאס מאראב׳ייאס
(Las Aventuras de Alisia en el Paiz de las Maraviyas),
Alice in Ladino, tr. Avner Perez, 2016

Alisis pīdzeivuojumi Breinumu zemē,
Alice in Latgalian, tr. Evika Muizniece, 2015

Alicia in Terra Mirabili, *Alice* in Latin, tr. Clive Harcourt Carruthers, 2011

Aliciae per Speculum Trānsitus (Quaeque Ibi Invēnit),
Looking-Glass in Latin, tr. Clive Harcourt Carruthers, Forthcoming

Alisa-ney Aventuras in Divalanda, *Alice* in Lingua de Planeta (Lidepla), tr.
Anastasia Lysenko & Dmitry Ivanov, 2014

La aventuras de Alisia en la pais de mervelias,
Alice in Lingua Franca Nova, tr. Simon Davies, 2012

Alice ehr Eventüürn in't Wunnerland,
Alice in Low German, tr. Reinhard F. Hahn, 2010

Contoyrtyssyn Ealish ayns Çheer ny Yindyssyn,
Alice in Manx, tr. Brian Stowell, 2010

Ko Ngā Takahanga i a Ārihi i Te Ao Mīharo,
Alice in Māori, tr. Tom Roa, 2015

Dee Erläwnisse von Alice em Wundalaund,
Alice in Mennonite Low German, tr. Jack Thiessen, 2012

Auanturiou adelis en Bro an Marthou,
Alice in Middle Breton, tr. Herve Le Bihan & Herve Kerrain, Forthcoming

The Aventures of Alys in Wondyr Lond,
Alice in Middle English, tr. Brian S. Lee, 2013

L'Avventure d'Alice 'int' 'o Paese d' 'e Maraveglie,
Alice in Neapolitan, tr. Roberto D'Ajello, 2016

L'Aventuros de Alis in Marvoland, *Alice* in Neo, tr. Ralph Midgley, 2013

Elises Eventyr i Undernes Land: den første norske *Alice:*
Elise's Adventures in the Land of Wonders: the first Norwegian *Alice,*
Alice in Norwegian, ed. & tr. Anne Kristin Lande, 2016

Æðelgýðe Ellendæda on Wundorlande,
Alice in Old English, tr. Peter S. Baker, 2015

La geste d'Aalis el Païs de Merveilles,
Alice in Old French, tr. May Plouzeau, 2016

Alitjilu Palyantja Tjuta Ngura Tjukurmankuntjala (Alitji's Adventures
in Dreamland), *Alice* in Pitjantjatjara, tr. Nancy Sheppard, 2016

Alitji's Adventures in Dreamland: An Aboriginal tale inspired by
Alice's Adventures in Wonderland, adapted by Nancy Sheppard, 2016

Alice Contada aos Mais Pequenos,
The Nursery "Alice" in Portuguese, tr., Rogério Miguel Puga, 2015

Соня въ царствѣ дива (Sonia v tsarstvie diva):
Sonja in a Kingdom of Wonder,
Alice in facsimile of the 1879 first Russian translation, 2013

Охота на Снарка (Okhota na Snarka),
The Hunting of the Snark in Russian, tr. Victor Fet, 2016

Ia Aventures as Alice in Daumsenland,
Alice in Sambahsa, tr. Olivier Simon, 2013

Ocolo id Specule ed Quo Alice Trohv Ter,
Looking-Glass in Sambahsa, tr. Olivier Simon, 2016

'O Tāfaoga a 'Ālise i le Nu'u o Mea Ofoofogia,
Alice in Samoan, tr. Luafata Simanu-Klutz, 2013

Eachdraidh Ealasaid ann an Tìr nan Iongantas,
Alice in Scottish Gaelic, tr. Moray Watson, 2012

Alice's Adventchers in Wunderland,
Alice in Scouse, tr. Marvin R. Sumner, 2015

Mbalango wa Alice eTikweni ra Swihlamariso,
Alice in Shangani, tr. Peniah Mabaso & Steyn Khesani Madlome, 2015

Ahlice's Aveenturs in Wunderlaant,
Alice in Border Scots, tr. Cameron Halfpenny 2015

Alice's Mishanters in e Land o Farlies,
Alice in Caithness Scots, tr. Catherine Byrne 2014

Alice's Adventirs in Wunnerlaun,
Alice in Glaswegian Scots, tr. Thomas Clark, 2014

Ailice's Anters in Ferlielann,
Alice in North-East Scots (Doric), tr. Derrick McClure, 2012

Alice's Adventirs in Wonderlaand,
Alice in Shetland Scots, tr. Laureen Johnson, 2012

Ailice's Àventurs in Wunnerland,
Alice in Southeast Central Scots, tr. Sandy Fleemin, 2011

Ailis's Anterins i the Laun o Ferlies,
Alice in Synthetic Scots, tr. Andrew McCallum, 2013

Alice's Carrànts in Wunnerlan,
Alice in Ulster Scots, tr. Anne Morrison-Smyth, 2013

Alison's Jants in Ferlieland,
Alice in West-Central Scots, tr. James Andrew Begg, 2014

Alice muNyika yeMashiripiti,
Alice in Shona, tr. Shumirai Nyota & Tsitsi Nyoni, 2015

Алисаньщ қайгаллыг Черинде полган чоруқтары
(Alisanyñ qaygallyg Çerinde polğan çoruqtarı),
Alice in Shor, tr. Liubov' Arbachakova, 2016

Alis bu Cëlmo dac Cojube w dat Tantelat,
Alice in Ṣurayt, tr. Jan Beṭ-Ṣawoce, 2015

Alisi Ndani ya Nchi ya Ajabu, *Alice* in Swahili, tr. Ida Hadjuvayanis, 2015

Alices Äventyr i Sagolandet, *Alice* in Swedish, tr. Emily Nonnen, 2010

'Alisi 'i he Fonua 'o e Fakaofo',
Alice in Tongan, tr. Siutāula Cocker & Telesia Kalavite, 2014

Ventürs jiela Lälid in Stunalän, *Alice* in Volapük, tr. Ralph Midgley, 2016

Lès-avirètes da Alice ô payis dès mèrvèyes,
Alice in Walloon, tr. Jean-Luc Fauconnier, 2012

Anturiaethau Alys yng Ngwlad Hud, *Alice* in Welsh, tr. Selyf Roberts, 2010

I Avventur de Alis ind el Paes di Meravili,
Alice in Western Lombard, tr. GianPietro Gallinelli, 2015

Di Avantures fun Alis in Vunderland,
Alice in Yiddish, tr. Joan Braman, 2015

Alises Avantures in Vunderland,
Alice in Yiddish, tr. Adina Bar-El, Forthcoming

Insumansumane Zika-Alice,
Alice in Zimbabwean Ndebele, tr. Dion Nkomo, 2015

U-Alice Ezweni Lezimanga, *Alice* in Zulu, tr. Bhekinkosi Ntuli, 2014

www.ingramcontent.com/pod-product-compliance
Lightning Source LLC
Chambersburg PA
CBHW022059050726

47591CB00002B/607